# Southbound Birds

## By Janetta Fudge Messmer

Angela:

Life is an adventure!

Janetta Fudge Messmer

Copyright © **2016  Janetta -Messmer**
**Published by: Forget Me Not Romances, a division of Winged**
**Publications**

ISBN-10:1-944203-69-9

ISBN-13:978-1-944203-69-6

PRAISE FOR EARLY BIRDS
Book One

*From the minute I met Janetta Messmer, I knew I would love her writing. Why? Because I adored her. Quirky. Funny. Poignant. A little kooky. . .she was my kind of girl. I read her wonderful story, Early Birds, and loved it so much. In fact, I almost felt as if I was traveling with Betsy and Ben in their RV. Fast-paced and fun, this novel is sure to delight all readers, particularly those in their middle-to-golden years. Be on the lookout for tender moments, as well as hilarious. Highly recommended!* - **Janice Thompson**, author of the *Weddings by Bella* series

*Janetta Fudge-Messmer doesn't write comedy. She lives it. The comic upturns and downturns of her own wackadoodle life are her inspiration. She's brilliantly funny, both in person and on the page.--* **Linda Kozar,** author of *When the Fat Ladies Sing cozy mystery series*

# ACKNOWLEDGEMENTS

*To my Lord and Savior. Couldn't do this writing thing without You in my life.*

*Also, to my hubby, Ray. You're the best CEO of Marketing and Daily Operations anyone could ask for. Almost every day you make me laugh and I sit in amazement at the brilliant ideas you come up with. But most of all, I'm over the moon that I get to share this On the Road Again adventure with you, my most favorite bud (and Maggie too). Love ya!!!*

CHAPTER ONE

Rose Wilford fumed and fussed in the passenger seat of their RV after she heard the scandalous news. How could Betsy do this to her? Her bestest friend in the whole wide world betrayed her. Then it hit her. "There's not a doubt in my mind."

"About what?"

"Larry, when I want you to hear something, all I hear is, "Huh". When I'm talking to myself—praise the angels of heaven—your ears are as wide open as the Red Sea when the Israelites went through it."

"Selective hearing, most of the time." Larry smiled at her. "But the way you said it, I thought you were talking to me. Anyway, what don't you have a doubt about?"

"The reason Bets is going to drive their albatross. Ben's offered to take her on the 15-night cruise she told me about the other day. It's out of Ft. Lauderdale. Said she wanted to get started on writing the book we talked about on our way back from Colorado."

"You're wrong on this one, sweetums. Ben would have asked us to take care of Matilda if a cruise was in their future."

"You're absolutely right. Ben's never one to leave any detail until the last minute." Rose fell silent, trying to think of another angle to this latest mystery with her friend. Nothing concrete came to mind as to why Betsy picked now to drive their truck with the trailer attached.

"Let's say we forego elaborate vacations for a second." Larry cleared his throat before he continued. "What if Betsy had a change of heart? Maybe the Lord convicted her with such force for not driving, she had no other choice?"

"I see where you're going with this, and I'm still not driving ours. If you, Larry Wilford, weren't driving, I'd...I don't know what I'd do."

Rose decided to laugh at what her hubby said despite the fact she'd rather have clobbered him, which then led to one of her famous snorts. The sad part, the truth of what he said outweighed the comedic aspect of it. No one coerced Betsy into doing anything she didn't want to do.

Joyce, at their home church in Texas, found out first hand when she'd asked Betsy to do a talk on inspirational blog writing. You'd have thought the Bible study leader suggested she sing the National Anthem at the upcoming Super Bowl, instead of sharing her writing with the group.

Betsy's exact words, "I write, therefore I don't have to speak in public."

*Someday, my friend, you'll eat those words – if and when you publish the book you keep talking about.*

Rose put those thoughts away and said, "Lar, you are right. The Lord did some talking to Betsy on this one. And, I'm proud of her for taking this task on. Ben will be safer with her behind the wheel."

"Say what? Are you telling me Ben isn't a safe driver?"

"The few times you've let him lead, I became a praying lunatic." Rose bowed her head for effect, even though she hoped Larry didn't look her way to see what she'd done.

"Explain yourself, dear."

"Instead of the saying, and I'm making another reference to Moses who said, 'Let my people go,' Ben needs to say, 'Let the people on the highway.' Or at least the ones trying to merge onto the road next to him. Get over, for goodness sakes."

"To come to his defense, you can't always get over when someone's trying to merge. You'd know this if you ever drove."

"I'll ignore your little jab, Mr. Wilford. I also know you can't always get over. In your case, I've learned to shut my eyes in those circumstances."

"It's show time."

"What?" Rose looked out of the windshield and saw the exit where Betsy would take over the reins. And where she'd pray for her best bud, before Bets kicked off her driving extravaganza on a portion of I-10.

***

"In Jesus Name. Amen." Rose hugged Betsy and stepped toward their truck. "You'll do fine driving. I'll keep praying for you all the way."

"Bets, I believe you're covered in plenty of prayers." Larry glanced at his watch. "Now it's time we get on the road again."

"You can never pray too many prayers," Betsy said as she headed to the driver's side of their truck. "And, Rose, thanks for the hugs, too."

"Want another one?"

"No she doesn't," Ben answered for his wife. "And, as Lar said, we need to get going. If we don't, we'll end up staying in Lake Charles tonight."

"Ben, I'd say your mood should spiffy up a piece." Rose walked over to him and pinched his cheek. "Let your Happy Camper shine. For the next however many miles your wife drives, you get to sit back and enjoy the scenery."

"Good point."

"Unlike the driver of the other 5th wheel sitting here at Pilot. I'm pretty sure I'd have a better disposition if you drove, too." Larry winked at his wife.

"We'll talk later. Right now, let's hit the road, so we can get to Baton Rouge. I want to hear Betsy's take on hauling their big rig down the highway."

"Rosie, you'll be the first to know. That is after Ben helps me pry my white-knuckled fingers off the steering wheel."

"Bets, you'll do great. Come on, Rosie. We're leading the way."

Larry got in and started their dually, after he scooted their pint-size pooch off his seat.

"Come here Baby. Sit on Mama's lap." Rose patted the side of her leg.

The Lhasa Apso ignored her invitation and took off for the back seat of the truck, yapping and growling with each step she took.

"Does that dog ever not make a ruckus?"

"Not since I've known her. But Larry look at her now. No…don't look, you're driving. She's lying on her pillow. Her paws are crossed. Like she's praying."

"She's praying I don't leave her at the next rest area."

"You'd do no such thing."

"No, but I'm tempted. Maybe I'd leave both of you there."

"Is that so?"

Larry thought that might be the only way he'd live through the moment when Rosie found out he knew about Betsy driving. How he'd helped Ben teach Betsy to drive when they landed back in Texas the month before.

His wife went to get her hair done one day and the lessons began. The next time, during one of Rose's doctor's appointments. The three of them found a parking lot for Betsy to practice driving.

After the lesson, Betsy said, "I'll never take the wheel, but I need to know how to. Just in case."

The never-say-never time had come. Larry didn't ask Ben when they stopped why his wife decided to take over, but knew he'd find out later.

He'd also ask him about the on ramp they'd passed ten miles back. Get his take on the close call. No doubt, that one changed Betsy's mind. Not sure how his friend's 5er and the sedan didn't kiss each other. Somehow the smaller of the two merged in time and got out of the way.

*Thankfully Rosie missed the whole fiasco.*

"Lar, I've been watching you since we got back on I-10. You're obviously not telling me something."

"Never, sweetheart. I tell you everything."

"Why don't I believe you?"

"I don't know."

Larry hoped he sounded convincing. But from the expression on Rose's face, when he glanced over at her shouted, "I'm not buying what you're selling."

"Try again, Larry."

He hemmed and hawed then thought he better tell her and get

the agony over with. His saving grace—he sat behind the wheel. She'd refrain from killing him while he drove down the major highway.

"Rosie, I sort of kept something from you the last couple of weeks."

"You've fallen off the wagon and are back gambling online again. I knew it."

"It's not that."

"Oh no. You've graduated and you're into p—"

"Never happen."

"Well, what is it then?"

Larry stayed silent, hoping for the Lord's return. Betsy had used that excuse a couple of times and it delayed the inevitable. Why not give it a try now?

"So, what is it? You're stalling and you know that can't be a good thing. For either one of us."

"Okay. I'm going to tell you. While we were in Texas, Ben and I took Bets out and taught her how to drive their dually with the 5er attached."

"How? When? Why didn't I know that?"

"We thought it best to keep it from you."

"I'll leave that statement alone, but I am confused. Why'd she tell me she'd never drive, make me think she's my ally, then change her mind today?"

"I'm not sure why she's driving, hon, and I'm sorry we kept it from you. That's not nice on our part."

"No, kind of feels like I got set up. But I am glad Bets didn't get behind the wheel still wet behind the ears."

"The other drivers out on the road are happy about it too."

"Preach it, brother. And while we're on the subject of keeping something from someone." Rose gave a little cough.

"Who might that be?"

"Moi."

"Spill it, Rosie."

Larry waited. He couldn't imagine what his wife hadn't told him and wasn't sure he wanted to know.

"Well, I...sort of...spent some money on an activity. Not really something you'll enjoy, but Betsy will almost wet her pants when she finds out."

In three sentences, Larry knew even less than before. Other than the fact his wife's friend might need a change of clothes when she found out about it. He'd wait. If he tried to rush her, it'd be even longer before he knew the answer.

"Aren't you going to ask me? Why you wouldn't care and Betsy would?"

"Okay, why don't I care about whatever it is and your BFF will? Not sure where Ben comes in on all this."

"He doesn't. He'll be at the concert with us."

"Concert?"

"Glad you asked. I've got tickets to see Willie Nelson in Biloxi, Mississippi on Saturday. Gives us four days to get there, get settled in and for me to figure out a way to get us backstage to talk to him."

*This can't be good.*

"Rose, you do realize that Willie is a big star and has very large body guards, making sure crazy people – you and Betsy – don't storm the stage?"

"I'm aware of Guido and Tiny, or whatever their names are. However, they've never met Rose Wilford."

"I'll give you that one."

More responses did the country swing on Larry's tongue, but he remained silent. No, Willie or his roadies had never met his wife, and if anyone could get anywhere on or behind the stage, Rosie would give it her best shot to get it done.

But why? Dare he ask? Since it sounded like money out of their account Larry asked, "And the reason we're seeing him is…?"

"Betsy has decided to write a book about all of us RVing. Willie's song, *On The Road Again,* inspired her. By the time we hit Texas, on our way back from Colorado, I'd helped her plot out the book and I don't even know how to write.

"Betsy assured me she'll fictionalize the story, but did say we needed to become quirkier, so she can get more ideas."

"That won't be a problem for you, dear." Larry chuckled.

"Oddity falls off of your family tree too, but that discussion is for another day too. Right now, I need to pray, pray and pray some more for Betsy. Do what I said. She'd appreciate some divine intervention to help her drive."

"Good idea, Rosie. And I won't say anything to Bets about your big surprise."

"Thanks, sweetie."

Larry left his wife to her prayer time and concentrated on the road. Louisiana's I-10 never changed. It still needed resurfaced in spots. On almost every overpass they went over, the connection on the truck and 5th wheel made a loud thud, which could wake the dead.

"Breaker 21."

"I can read you."

"Betsy's had enough. There's a truck stop at the next exit in Lafayette."

"I'll take it."

Larry made the turn into Pilot and parked, leaving Betsy plenty of room to pull in behind him. As he came to a stop he said, "Rosie, you better get out and give Bets a hug. I'll bet she needs one about now."

He didn't get the words out of his mouth before his wife jumped out of their truck. But before she slammed the door she turned and said, "Took the words right out of my mouth."

"I know her too well," Larry spoke the words in the empty truck and wondered why he sat there. He needed to get out there and find out how Betsy's first time behind the wheel went and how Ben handled the experience.

"You should have seen it. I'm coming up to the ramp. The car is com—"

"…coming down the ramp. Betsy checked the traffic in the mirror and she changed lanes like a pro."

"Ben, I appreciate your accolades, but before you get too excited I have to tell you something."

"What? Did you cut someone off when you changed lanes?" Ben's smile disappeared.

"No. Nothing like that. I want to tell you I'm sorry for harassing you about people merging. It's not as easy as it looks. Lots to think about and too many directions to check at one time."

"Thanks. That means a lot to me."

Larry watched his friends kiss and he prided Ben for not coming back with a smart remark. Not sure he'd kept quiet if Rosie had said the same to him. Sometimes harassing his wife seemed right.

*Maybe she doesn't do things because I'm always pestering her?*

"Old man are you going to get back in and drive or what?"

Larry observed the trio standing in front of him and laughed. "Having a conversation with myself. Do you mind?"

Ben stepped up and said, "I do when we're trying to make it somewhere before dark."

"I have an idea." Larry turned to face the front of the truck stop and pointed. "Lunch anyone?"

"I'm in." Ben headed across the parking lot and opened the door to their favorite restaurant. Taco Bell.

Larry followed, chiming in with "Me too" then heard a chorus of, "Me three" and "Me four" from the ladies following behind him. At that moment he realized they missed the other two Early Birds and said as much.

"Me five and me six. That's for Jeff and Mary."

"Oh my goodness. I can't believe we won't see them until we hit Florida." Rose took her phone out. "Got a text from Mary this morning. She said the paperwork should be finished the first of next week. Then they're on the road to meet up with us."

Another holler went up among the foursome and before Larry got the masses quieted, he saw everyone staring at them from inside the eatery. Ben came to their rescue and said, "Ladies and gentlemen, it's time to order lunch."

They did and when the female employee called their numbers, Ben went to get it. He set it down, but before they took their first bite Rosie asked, "So, Betsy, do we need to have your blood pressure checked? You're a little pale after your big adventure. Ben, lean over and give your honey a smooch. That'll bring her color back."

After the laughter died down Ben complied, giving his wife a kiss on the lips. He sat back in his chair and said, "Anything I can do to help."

"You done good, Benjamin. I can see her color returning." Rose unwrapped her burrito and added. "Bets is among the living again."

"Yes, I am. And truth be told, Rosie, my lack of skin tone came from the sendoff you gave me before I got in the truck to drive. I figured you'd never talk to me again. Let alone hug me."

"Bets, all I could do was hug you. You flat bumfuggled me when you said you were going to take the wheel. Today you renamed Carrie Underwood's song. It's now called, *With the Lord's Help, Betsy Took the Wheel.*" Rose slapped her leg and her customary noise followed.

"That's not the half of it. During the hairy time Ben told you about, I'm pretty sure Jesus didn't just take the wheel, He sat smack dab on my lap, making sure the truck and trailer stayed steady."

"And, Betsy, with that declaration, I'm pretty sure you're hitting the hooch."

"Ladies, whatever Jesus chooses to do is fine with me, but I'm pretty sure if we continue this conversation we'll never get on the road again."

"But before we do that, hon, I have to find out why my best friend didn't tell me about learning to drive."

"Ben, we might as well pitch a tent. This could take a while."

"Yep."

Rose put down her burrito and said, "Bets, my hubby told me all about how you three conspired against me in Texas."

"Conspired is a strong word, Rosie. What I'd call it is we planned to tell you, even when we were in The Woodlands, but it never seemed the right time."

"Since this is coming from you, I'll consider its validity. However, next time, I'd like to be privy to any monkeyshine that's going on behind my back."

"Monkeyshine?"

"Yessiree! Monkeyshine is my new word of the day."

"Back to what we were talking about, Rose, if I had told you, you'd have tried to talk me out of it. Isn't that true?"

"Not a doubt in my mind."

"Can I tell you something, Rosie?"

"Sure."

She held her breath, afraid her best friend would tell her she hated driving and she and Ben decided to quit RVing.

"I hate to admit it, but it's fun driving the monster. Don't recommend a person to take over driving without practicing first, but with what the guys showed me, which helped immensely, it's actually a kick in the pants."

"I'll take your word for it." Rose smiled and proceeded to take another bite of her bean burrito.

While they ate, a discussion about their travel plans to Baton Rouge ensued and Ben said, "MapQuest says we're on the fastest route." He put his phone on the table. "It says we're fifty-nine miles away."

"Why didn't you tell me to keep driving?"

"And miss this fine fare?"

"Larry, one day the Lord is going to smite you for fibbing. How about we hush and enjoy our meal?"

The foursome dug in and silence filled their space until Betsy said, "Did anyone see the billboard for Willie Nel—"

From the other side of the table Rose made a snort/cough/gurgle noise and Larry thought at first she'd choked on her food. Then he realized her fit most likely came from what her friend said. He wanted to laugh, but saw Ben and Betsy's eyes zeroed in on his wife.

Larry watched as Rosie's choking subsided, but became concerned when her coloring hit a hue of light pinkish on its way to a fiery red tone.

"Waatteer."

Larry shot up and came back with a glass of cold water to calm the trauma going on with his wife. "Hon, is that better," Lar said with a wink.

"Remind me never to try the Fire sauce ever again." Rose smiled at him.

"I hear they're coming out with the Diablo. 'Hottest Sauce Yet' according to Huffington Post." This time Ben put his phone in his pocket.

"Dear, you do store a bevy of superfluous information inside that brain of yours, don't you?" Betsy asked then took a bite of her burrito.

"I do, with Google's help. How about we finish here and hit the highway? I'm not sure I mentioned this, but I made the reservations for Baton Rouge before we left Houston. The woman said there'd be plenty of room. Only issue, they're back-in spots."

Larry wadded up his wrapper and tossed it in the sack and said, "Since I'm the skilled one at parking, I'll show you the ropes."

"Do I need to remind you I'm not the one who almost sideswiped a pole in Denver."

"He's got you there, dear."

They finished their meals and the Early Birds made their way across the parking lot. Larry hurried to his truck and got in. After shutting his door, he rolled down the window and yelled, "What are you waiting on, Rosie? Are you riding with Ben and Betsy?"

"Don't give me an option."

Larry pulled away from his parking spot, moving at a snail's pace. He kept his eyes on the driver's mirror, wanting to see his wife's reaction to him moving forward. A few more feet.

*Why is Rose waving?*

Clunk!

"What in blue blazes?"

Larry slammed on the brakes and spotted the light pole. The right corner of his dually sat against it. To add to the mix, Baby stood on his shoulder and yelped in his left ear.

"Are you okay?" Rose asked as she came up to his opened window.

"No I'm not. Get in and don't say a word. Please."

Larry got out and surveyed the scene. The others stayed out of his way, which made him extremely happy. No need for any of them to hear his choice words for running into one more thing.

*Lord, I'm about ready to park this monstrosity. Do You hear me?*

"Hey, bud, is there anything I can do to help?" Ben walked up and stood beside him.

"Not really." Larry took his sunglasses off and wiped them on his t-shirt. "Yes, Ben, there is something. Teach me not to play around when I get behind the wheel of this thing."

"We've all done stupid things." Ben walked up closer to the truck. "Do you need to call your insurance?"

"Nah. Not enough damage for it to matter."

"Are you ready to go?"

"Yes, but I'll let you lead the way. Obviously, I'm not doing a very good job."

"Remember what you tell Betsy—don't be too hard on yourself."

"That doesn't count when you embarrass yourself like I did a few minutes ago."

"I'll pray harder for you tonight." Ben laughed and turned to go to his truck. Before he got to it he turned and said, "Lar, you are fun to watch sometimes."

"As Rosie says, 'Glad I could entertain you.' I think it's time to get going."

"Yes, sir."

Larry jumped in and noticed Rose staring at him and he asked, "Would you get it over with. I deserve whatever you have to say."

"I love you and I'm sorry for the boo boo on your truck."

"So am I, dear. So am I. And I'm glad you squelched the subject of Willie so brilliantly."

"We are a pair, aren't we?"

"That we are, my dear."

CHAPTER TWO

The Atchafalaya Swamp, visible on both sides of the truck, amazed Rosie and caused her to ask Larry the same question she always asked when they went over it. "Hon, how did the State of Louisiana build I-10 over these alligator-infested waters?"

"They built it the same way as I told you the other half a dozen times we've been on this highway. It hasn't changed."

"My, Larry, you're quite the cranky pants this afternoon."

"Running into light poles would have the same effect on most people."

"You didn't even scratch the truck."

Rose thought if she reasoned with her hubby it'd ease his discomfort. It didn't. If anything, it made it worse.

"What difference does it make whether there is or isn't a dent. Or if the front fender fell off completely. I HIT the pole."

With each word Larry uttered, Rose noticed his hands tightened more and more on the steering wheel.

*Thank goodness the sentence isn't ten words long.*

"Rosebud, that smile you're wearing better not have to do with me trying to mow down a utility pole."

A snort came out of Rose before she could stop it. She covered her mouth, but that made even more noise. The harder she tried to contain herself, the worse it got.

"Fine. Laugh all you want. Glad I can be the butt of everyone's jokes. This tops Ben and his charade in Colorado Springs, doesn't it?"

"Lar, I'm sorry. I don't mean to laugh at you. But when you do something, you do it up right and usually in front of a crowd."

Larry glanced over to Rose. "There wasn't anyone else out in the parking lot when it happened."

"Is that a question or a statement?"

"However you want to take it."

"I'll take it as a question. Yes, Larry, by the time you moved the RV, there was quite the crowd gathered outside the truck stop. If you'd been listening, I'm sure you got a standing ovation for your grand exit."

"I'll be sure to ask Ben if we had an audience. Not sure I'll take your word for it. You could be lying to me."

"Now that's an interesting concept. I could say the same about the other three Early Birds. Not telling me the truth about Betsy learning to drive. I still don't know how you accomplished the task without me knowing about it?"

"Between all your appointments. We had time to teach Bets all she needed to know about driving a big rig."

"After what happened with the pole, that's kind of scary." Rose snickered.

"Got a point there."

"Is that a smile, I see?" Rose reached over and touched her husband's shoulder. "I love this guy much more than the Mr. Crabby Pants of a few minutes ago."

"If you like this Larry so much better, can you do me a favor?"

Rose knew she'd regret saying what came out, but she said it anyway. "I'll do whatever you need."

"I want you to drive from now on."

Rosie wanted to give her hubby one of her five basic looks, but knew clear down to her very soul it wouldn't solve their recurring problem. The only two things capable of resolving it— prayer and do what Betsy had done a few hours earlier. Drive this PUPPY!

*Oh Lord, have mercy on me.*

"Still over there, Rosie?"

"I am. And I'm praying for the Lord to protect you from me."

"Thought so."

***

Larry thought about his wife's somewhat truthful statement as he drove along I-10. As well as he knew his Rosie, she hadn't been praying for his demise, but for a solution. The same she'd done throughout their marriage.

No denying her faithfulness to pray for him and their relationship. It had saved them from many scrimmages. But this one with driving might take the Lord coming down and putting tape on his mouth and sitting Rose in the driver's seat to get it accomplished.

This revelation caused Larry to chuckle, which made his bride look to her left. Her mouth opened to say something, but before she could ask him the reason for his amusement he said, "Rosebud, you do know I'm not mad at you. All I'm asking is for some help driving. That's all."

"I'm working on it."

"Sure you are?"

Larry's attempt at brevity fell off the edge of the cliff after hearing Rosie's curt answer of, "I think it's time I pray again", told him he'd questioned her faith and her fingers around his neck might be her next move.

"Yes, dear. One of your hit-heaven-between-the-eyes prayers would fit the bill right about now."

The love of his life took off on such a prayer and Larry imagined the angels of the Lord carrying them and their 5th wheel down the Louisiana highway. He also suspected some of Rosie's words came through gritted teeth. But all in all, her prayer touched his heart.

*She is working on it. Thank You, Lord.*

Larry drove in silence the last few miles and when Ben took the exit off I-10, he followed him to the Shady Glen RV Park. They checked in and Curtis guided Ben to their spot. He watched his friend park and then he hopped out, holding Matilda in his arms.

Curtis came over to Larry's window and said, "Sir, it's your turn."

Once again the stars aligned…but not in a good way. As Larry backed up, the 5<sup>th</sup> wheel wouldn't cooperate. He pulled forward, straightened it out and tried again. Still it stayed on the wrong course.

Before Larry figured out he had a problem, and while he yelled at Rose to put the CB mic down, he heard a noise and someone yelling, "Stop. Now."

"Oh no, hon, I think you ran over something." Rose jumped out of the truck after he stopped.

Larry put his truck in gear and then ran back and joined his wife and Curtis at the rear of their trailer.

"I yelled for you to stop, Mr. Wilford. You must not have heard me."

"It's my fault. I had the CB on. Didn't hear you until…"

Larry's blood pressure spiked, which told him and everyone else who watched him that he'd better sit down ASAP or they'd find him sprawled out on the ground, needing medical attention.

He took a seat on a tree stump and raised his arm, straight up over his head. Rose rushed over to him. "Are you okay? Can you hear me?"

"I'm going to live."

He watched his wife as she stepped back and Larry thought he heard a tiny snort before she continued, "Lar, I need to ask. Why in heaven's name is your right arm flapping in the breeze?"

"You told me to put my arm in the air the other day at Walgreens. That it would help lower my blood pressure. I thought you were being a tad wacky, but today I decided to give it a shot."

"I told you to put your hand up when you heard our name called. When it was our turn to talk to the pharmacist."

"Is that what you meant?"

"That's not important. Are you sure you're okay?"

"I will be when I find out what happened." Larry took a drink out of the bottled water Curtis gave him then returned to the back of their 5<sup>th</sup> wheel. Ben, Betsy and Rose tagged along—for support, he hoped.

"Lar, the bad news is the back of your trailer has a scratch on it."

"What's the good news, Ben?"

"It's only a half inch scratch on the back of your trailer." Ben added, "And, the picnic table you hit, did not puncture the siding."

"Mr. Wilford, again, I'm so sorry."

"Please call me Larry and this isn't your fault." Larry peered over his glasses at his beloved who stood next to him.

"Yes, it's all my fault. I know better than to fiddle around with things when he's trying to park."

"What exactly were you doing with the CB anyway, my love?"

"I made up my own little song for when we land at an RV Park. Wanted everyone to hear it as we pulled in? Do you want me to sing it?"

"Sure thing. My day can't get much worse."

"I cheated and used the music to *On the Road Again,* but changed the words." Rose took out a piece of paper, cleared her throat and sang a couple of "Me, Me, Mes" before belting out, "At the park again. Just can't wait to get settled at a new park again."

"I've heard enough. Ben, do you want to help me move the table back where it belongs?"

"No, I want to hear this song in its entirety." He stopped when laughter took over his words.

Betsy, who appeared as if she tried to get control of herself said, "Please let her keep going. This is priceless."

With her friend's prompting, Rose went on. "The life I love is camping with my friends...that was until a few minutes ago."

Rose quit serenading them and waltzed over to the picnic table Larry assaulted earlier. She'd sit and stew about her part in said crime and stay out of everybody's way.

"Are you done, Rosebud?"

"Yes, and honey, I'm really sorry about all this with the trailer. I promise I won't make a peep while you're parking again."

"Hon, let's talk about this later. I'm sure Curtis would like to go back to work and not stand here listening to us all day."

"If you're wife's singing anymore of the song, I'm all ears."

"Please don't encourage her, Curtis. She's hard enough to live with as it is."

Curtis laughed and then he took one more look around where Larry pulled in. "Mr. Wilford, this isn't your fault. The table wasn't where it was supposed to be. I should check out the site before telling you to back in. We'll pay for the damages to your trailer."

Dumbfounded at the man's words, Larry uttered a simple, "Thank you."

Curtis tipped his straw hat and ambled off toward the maintenance garage. Larry took a deep breath and for a short second he imagined what could have happened to their truck and 5$^{th}$ wheel that day. He thanked God for the minor damage and that no one got hurt.

Other than his pride. AGAIN.

## CHAPTER THREE

Later in the evening Rosie scrolled through Facebook and fretted over the trailer and table collision she'd caused. As she started to go past one of the many sayings on her screen, she stopped and read, "Faith moves mountains. Fear creates them."

Rosie grabbed her phone and texted the profound words to Betsy and added, "You moved your mountain (driving) today. Now it's my turn…your friend says while shaking in her pretty pink cowboy boots. "

Seconds later Rose's phone buzzed and she clicked on Betsy's text. "No need to shake. You'll learn in due time. Love your song by the way. And love ya, too."

When her friend ended her correspondence with, "Love ya" it meant she'd shut off her phone for the night. No more discussion on aforementioned text. Until tomorrow. Or never.

"Fine with me, Bets. If you don't want to discuss my phobia in depth tonight. Call it what it is. I'm a fraidy cat. There I said it." Rose laughed at her own admission.

"What's so funny?" Larry walked into their bedroom. "Did I hear you talking to someone?"

"I'm simply analyzing myself since Betsy's too busy writing her novel. I'm small peanuts now."

Larry came and sat down on the edge of the bed. "Got a

question for you, dear, is Bets going to add my two little fiascos from earlier into her story? I hope she gets the song right that you sang. Don't want anyone to miss out on that little gem."

"As I said before, I'm really sorry. It'll never happen again."

"No it won't since I'm turning the truck keys over to you. As of tonight. You better enjoy the next few days here in Baton Rouge. When we take off on Wednesday morning—you're driving."

"Next few days? Aren't we leaving tomorrow?"

"Nope."

Rose's own blood pressure, heart rate and the urge to move to Afghanistan almost overtook her sensibility. It also muted her ability to form words. Thank goodness. Since what she wanted to say would have more than smoothed out the crow's feet next to Larry's baby blues.

"And furthermore, Rosebud, I'm serious about giving you the keys. I also made an appointment at Frontier RV for you to get driving lessons tomorrow morning." Larry turned around and stomped down the stairs.

*Oh my! Oh my! Oh my!*

Rosie texted Bets. Certain she'd get her support and some tactics she'd give her to use to talk Larry out of this preposterous plan. But no answer came, even after giving her friend over two minutes to answer.

"Lights are out over at the Stevenson's."

"I see that."

"Why don't you and Baby come down? Watch the news with me? We can cuddle in front of the fireplace?"

*Over my dead body.*

But then again, maybe this could work to her advantage. Maybe she'd be able to talk him out of this stupid idea he'd come up with.

*Maybe…*

Rose sashayed down the two steps, carrying their pooch, and they joined Larry on their couch.

"Thanks for the invite."

"Sure thing."

"Lar, are you feeling okay?"

"Uh huh."

"Are you sure?"

"Never been better." Larry put his arm around Rose.

She snuggled in closer to her husband and said, "This is nice." And she meant every word, but her next statement almost stopped the earth's spin. "Lar, if I give you back your iPad, so you can play your games, will you promise not to make me learn how to drive?"

Laughter erupted to her right and Rose calculated her hubby didn't breathe for a good forty-five seconds. When he took in some air he said, "You can't be serious?" Larry scooted over. "I'm pretty sure the Lord didn't prompt you to make that arrangement."

"No. And you should have put your hand on my forehead and said, 'Satan, get behind this crazy woman.'"

"That's more like it. I'm glad the Rosie I married is back. Not too fond of the one making deals with the devil. How about we head for bed? It's been a long day."

"Go on. I'll be there in a minute."

Rose intended to read the verses she'd underlined in her Bible about anxiety and fear, but her mind kept going back to what she'd said to her hubby. She took out her journal and wrote, "Lord, I know I'm fearfully and wonderfully made, but tonight the clay vessel you created is an insensitive clod of dirt. Please help me take Larry's feelings into account more often and not my own. AMEN."

She shut her book and put it and her Bible next to the couch. After checking on their coffee supply for morning, Rose walked upstairs and settled in beside Baby and Larry. A growl came from their furry yapper, but after she petted her, their dog relaxed and went back to sleep.

Unlike her pooch, slumber eluded Rose and counting sheep didn't work either. So instead of getting up and waking the household, she decided she'd pray through the alphabet. A hint she'd seen on Facebook.

*A – Apple. Apple? Lord, do You want me to pray for the corporation or for the fruit?*

Rose chuckled at the thought and couldn't imagine what would pop into her head next, but by the sounds of it—it'd be a long night

***

Larry fiddled with the back compartment door he'd damaged

the day before. After a pull or two, it opened. He checked the lock mechanism and found it had turned. A screwdriver and a few twists on the screw fixed it. The small scratch ended up the only thing to contend with.

*Considering all that happened yesterday, I'm a happy guy.*

However, over coffee, Rose had said, "You're a testy mess."

He wanted to respond with, "Takes one to know one", but he refrained. No need to start another argument. Instead, Larry picked up his coffee and went outside. "A testy mess indeed. Why shouldn't I be?"

"Shouldn't be what?" Ben queried when he walked up with Matilda.

"Never mind. Not worth talking about. Anyway, I'm leaving it in the Lord's hands."

"And making an appointment at the RV place for Rose to learn how to drive? Not sure that's leaving it in the Lord's hands."

"There's no appointment for anything. I told Rosie she had one to get her riled." Larry laughed.

"Rose is more than riled, but it seems it's more at herself than you. When I saw her a few minutes ago she mumbled something about almost signing a deal with the devil. What's going on, Larry?"

He told Ben what happened the night before and added, "I still can't believe she tried to make that bargain with me. How did I know that asking her to drive would upset her so much?"

"I guess we can't blame her, or Betsy. If you remember right, I wasn't too fond of trying to maneuver the beast either."

"But you learned. She should too."

"I agree with you, but you DO need to leave this one with the Lord. Or, it's going to make all of us VERY unhappy campers."

"I hate when you're right. Guess it's time to tell Rose she doesn't have to learn to drive."

"Good idea."

*For the time being, that is...sorry Lord.*

They found their wives huddled together in the Stevenson's living room. Praying. Heads down. A coming together Jesus meeting.

*This is serious.*

"...I leave all of this in Your hands, Lord. In Jesus Name.

Amen." Rose closed out the prayer time and glanced over at Larry and said, "Is it time?"

After that last comment, Larry wanted with every amount of his being to carry on the charade, but the stare down he got from Ben told him to rethink his plan.

"No, honey, it's not time. You don't have an appointment to learn anything. I was pulling your leg." Larry waited for the laughter and to hear how funny he was.

Neither came and he grimaced at the scowl his bride gave him. Larry backed into the tiny kitchen and wanted to wave a white flag in surrender, but didn't have one. Instead he said, "Okay, I screwed up. I'm sorry. That wasn't anything to tease about. I promise I'll never do it again."

Thinking he'd covered all the bases, he went over to Rose and gave her a hug. At which time she burst into tears and babbled on about something he couldn't make out. Larry glanced over at Ben and Betsy and they shrugged their shoulders.

Rose stepped away from Larry and said, "It's not that. You have nothing to apologize for, well…I can't say that honestly. What you did was underhanded, BUT what I asked you—it was wrong in soooooooo so sooooooooo many ways."

"No, just one area and talk about picking my chin up off the floor last night when you tried to make the deal with me. Still can't believe you said it."

"Lar, I'm with you. When she told me this morning what she did, I almost turned her around to see if she had a zipper."

"A zipper?" Ben, Larry and Rose said it at the same time.

"Yeah, a zipper. Like someone had come in and changed our Rosie out for her evil twin."

Laughter filled the Stevenson's RV and Larry thanked the Lord for friendship and a way out of a serious situation.

Yes, saying something ludicrous worked every time.

## CHAPTER FOUR

The next morning, after Larry gave Curtis his contact information, the Early Birds hugged before getting in their prospective RVs. As always, Rosie took their farewell twenty steps beyond normal.

Larry ignored his wife and got in their truck, depositing Baby in the back seat. For once the mutt kept quiet.

*Matilda must be rubbing off on you. Thank You, Jesus!*

Larry put on his seat belt and the CB crackled and Ben's voice sounded, "Breaker 21. We ready for takeoff?"

"Not until our wives find their seats."

"Could take all day." Ben laughed.

"You're telling me."

While they waited, Larry gave Ben the exit number for Biloxi. "We should arrive around noon. Unless we're detained by you know wh—"

"Who is here now. How about you put this thing in gear and get a move on?"

"Ben, you've heard the boss."

Larry headed down the merge lane onto I-10, but before all ten wheels hit the major highway the CB squawked again, "Breaker 21. We need to sing *On the Road Again.*"

"Let's not and say we did."

"Bets, don't listen to my hubby, but hold that thought. I need to talk with Lar. Be right back."

Rose turned in her seat and declared, "If we don't sing it, I'll grace the airways with my rendition I sang yesterday. If I change up a few words. What is it, buddy boo?"

"I prefer neither, but when you put it that way, I'll take Willie's every time."

"Good choice." Rose picked up the mic and said, "Breaker 21. We're on the road. Let's hit it."

Larry had to admit the foursome sounded a tad better, but on the second verse Baby joined in and her howls drowned everyone else out.

"We've slaughtered enough of the song. Talk to you later." Larry put the mic down and focused on driving.

"Can you believe in two days we're going to hear Willie Nelson sing the song in person. I can't wait."

"What I can't believe is that you've kept this secret from Betsy. She almost had you in Taco Bell."

"Almost. If my quick thinking hadn't kicked in, I'd have erupted like a volcano in the springtime. Or whenever they go off."

"Or me getting you a glass of water to save you from choking."

"A helpful thing and much appreciated. Anyway, this concert is sure to inspire Bets to write, write, write." Rose clapped her hands. "And if we get backstage, it'll be the topping on the tamale."

"As I told you the other day, don't count on getting back there."

"I know. I know. Willie's security team is tighter than any Spanx I've ever tried to shimmy into. But, there's always a way. You might need work to do it, but it's a relief when they're…" Rose quit talking then added. "Forget what I said. It didn't make a lick of sense."

Larry kept his eyes straight ahead, deciding that questioning what his wife meant would bring more discussion than he wanted. Rose must have felt the same. She took out the atlas next to her seat and settled it on her lap, turning pages and putting something in her phone.

"We went by the Stennis turn off a couple miles ago. Another forty miles to the Tadpole RV and Campground."

"Good. A few days there, near the water, will do us all good."

"If you say so."

"Sun. Surf. Sand. I can't wait to walk barefoot on the beach. Pick up shells. See some sunsets. Whatever the Lord has in store for the Early Birds. That's what's on my agenda. What's on yours?"

"Rose, I forgot to tell you, Ben talked to Tim at Flatirons Church in Colorado. He gave him someone to contact here in Biloxi to volunteer. We'll see if they need someone for a few days."

"I'm not sure, but I'm beginning to feel that our communication is lacking. Is there anything else you haven't told me?"

"No, that's all I have. You?"

"I'm good."

"Breaker 21."

"Betsy said we need the Biloxi exit. 46A."

"That's the one we're taking."

"As always, I'm right behind you."

"Ben, I'm going to start singing *Me and My Shadow*. Larry laid the mic down and laughed.

"No, you're not. Give me the mic." Rose took a piece of paper out of the side pocket of the door. "I'm going to sing all of us into our spot with the song I sang to you yesterday. Remember?"

"How could I forget and no, you're not." Larry grabbed the mic from its holder and stretched the cord out as far as it went and hid it in the side pocket of the truck. "You promised, and I have witnesses, that you'd be quiet. Don't need any interruptions while I'm parking."

"Okay, I won't make a peep."

"Bless you."

Larry turned off of I-10 and in a short while they hit Highway 90. The Gulf of Mexico glistened out in front of them. The sight almost deterred Rose's train of thought, but she soon had it back on track and said, "Since I'm an *interruption*, I'll jump out at the next light and hitch a ride with Ben & Betsy."

"Don't fall on your way out, since it's a ways down to the pavement."

Larry's comment caused Rose's snorts to hit a high note and

the noise continued all the way to the front gate of the campground. As her hubby pulled next to the office she said, "I'll be good…and quiet."

"I'm counting on it."

***

"I believe we hit the jackpot with these two spots." Larry pushed the button inside the compartment and the jacks leveled the 5th wheel on its own. "I do love how they work."

"Until they don't."

"What's going on, Ben?"

"Come over here and look."

Larry walked over to C14 and spied Ben's problem. "Looks like a hydraulic hose busted. Again."

His friend's sidelong glance and spots on his polo shirt told Larry he'd proclaimed the obvious. To save their friendship, he added, "Sorry. What can I do?"

"Find out from the office if they know of a place I can get a new hose made. I'll be here cleaning up."

Larry hurried to the office and the owner of the park gave him two numbers to call. While he called to set up an appointment, Ben conquered his oily mess inside his compartment. They headed out and almost made it a foot or two when Rose stopped their forward progress.

"Lar, hold on, Bets needs to get her swimming suit out of the 5er before you take it. We're goin' to the beach to bask in the 80 plus temperature. I've got my phone in case you need us."

"We'll be fine."

"Rose, when you're done, tell Bets to lock the door."

"Will do."

"Ben, I can see that your wife is concerned about your trailer." Larry smiled while they waited for the women to finish.

"Since it's happened before, it's old news."

"Yoo-hoo in there." Rose came up to the window. "You're free to go."

The two hit the road to find Randy's Hose and Supply. The closer they got to the industrial park, the less MapQuest made sense. Larry held up his friend's phone and said, "P.I.T.S. is recalculating for the fourth time."

"Make a U-turn," the voice on the phone repeated.

"See. What did I tell you?" Larry handed the phone to Ben and said, "She's confused."

"And she doesn't know what she's talking about. We need to make a right or left. Not a U-turn."

"Make a U-turn," the phone repeated herself.

Larry laughed. "She's pretty adamant about us following her directions."

"I have a better idea." He took his phone and turned the app off. "I'm going to give them a call. It's obviously a job for a human. Not technology."

Larry checked his emails while Ben called. He marked two from gaming sites as SPAM and moved on. The last one stopped him. Dr. LeRoy Tucker?

*What does he want?*

He clicked and read the email, "Dr. Tucker would like for you to make another appointment for a follow-up, concerning your blood pressure."

"Great."

Larry closed the email then opened his voicemail. He'd meant to check it the day before, after he missed a call, but when the number didn't show a person's name, he put it out of his mind.

Until now. He listened to the message. Nothing alarming to add to what the email said. He reopened the email again and reread it. Then deleted it. If Rosie saw it, she'd send the National Guard out for them before Ben got his hose made.

"Hey, did I lose you over there?"

"No, I'm here." Larry shut his phone off and put it in his pocket. "Did you figure out where this hose place is?"

"I did, but you look like someone died."

Larry leaned back and took a deep breath. "The doc in Houston wants me to do a follow up on my blood pressure. Guess I'll be doing it when I get to Ft. Myers."

"I'm sure with all the Snowbirds, there are plenty of doctors down there to choose from."

"Health concerns and traveling don't go hand in hand."

"Getting older doesn't sound like much fun. You are going to tell Rosie, aren't you?"

"If I didn't delete the email soon enough, she'll have seen it. A helicopter will be ready to take me to the Mayo Clinic when we make it home."

Ben laughed. "You need to tell her. If you keep one more piece of news from her, you'll need to be airlifted to the area hospital for head trauma."

"Do tell."

Larry had no intention of hiding this development from his wife. His only concern—she'd make a much bigger deal out of it than needed and said to Ben, "You are coming with me when I tell Rose. I'm not going in alone."

"No chance I'm missing this."

Their conversation ended when Ben pulled into the hose place. He and Larry joined Randy at the side compartment and the store owner measured the length needed for the replacement.

A half hour later, Ben got the hydraulic hose and they headed to the RV Park. On the way Larry commented, "You know in the city, this part would have ran you close to a hundred bucks. Not thirty-five dollars."

"I know and I can't believe Randy came in on his day off."

"How about we get this hose put on before the girls know we're back? I'm certain that Rosie will be chasing me down when she sees me."

Ben maneuvered his trailer into the spot and the two men made quick work of the hose installation. With the last clamp tightened, Larry wiped his hands on the towel he took out of his back pocket and announced, "We do good work."

"Yes, we do. An engineer and an architect. I can hear the joke now? They walk into a ba—"

"Baby. My sweet Baboo." Rose came charging out of their RV door. "You need to come inside and sit down. Let me take care of you."

Larry stuck his arm out to stop Rose from tackling him when she came down the stairs and rushed to his side. Her reaction didn't surprise him, but her exuberance told him she'd read the email and thought he had one leg in the grave and the other teetering on the edge.

"Why don't you guys come over here." Ben motioned for Betsy and they went up the steps and disappeared. Matilda, their pooch, stood at the door, jumping up and down.

"Mats, you're going to have to back away from the door and

let Larry inside. There's a sick person coming in." Rose stood at the bottom of the stairs, talking to the pooch. Matilda continued to hop around the door.

"Hon, I'm really okay." Larry heard laughter from the RV as he walked up the steps, past Matilda, and took a seat at the dining table across from Ben.

Once Rose made it inside, he watched as she fluffed a pillow on Betsy's loveseat and motioned for him to sit next to her.

"For the last time. I'm fine. Leave me alone."

Rose walked over to him and touched his forehead, "Lar, you're feeling a little warm."

"And, you're making more of this than—"

"Then what? You do know you can keel over from this. This is high blood pressure we're talking about. You didn't stub your toe." Rose wiped at the corner of her eye.

"Rosebud, there's no need to cry. I'm well aware I could kick off from this dreaded disease," He smiled and then continued. "And, I'm sure you'll remind me I'm inflicted with it more than once on our way to Florida."

"Go ahead, make jokes." Rose massaged his temples. "All I'm saying, Buster Brown, if you die…where…does that leave us?"

Before he could remark on what his wife said, she'd put her hand over her mouth. Larry wanted to laugh, but refrained when he saw her horrified look. At that moment he decided he'd better save her from any more quips that might spill out. But she beat him to it. Again.

"Larry, what I meant to say, you'd be missed. Wouldn't he, Ben and Betsy? You do know that, don't you?"

"Remember what Ben said to Betsy years ago. 'Now would be a good time for you to be quiet.'"

Rose smiled and opened the door. "Larry, it's time we go home."

"Couldn't agree more."

"S'mores. Did someone say my favorite word?"

"There he goes again, talking about food. Ben, is your leg hollow?"

"It is if it includes chocolate, marshmallows and Graham Crackers."

"Do people in Mississippi have fires? Isn't it too warm?"

"Rose, it's like Texas the end of October. If we wait until later tonight, it'll be cool enough."

"We'll meet you around 8:00. By then you and Rose will have kissed and made up."

"I'm not sure about that, Bets. Since my wife is planning my demise, I'll be coming over to your place later to sleep."

"Larry Wilford, it's high time you put a lid on it. I'm doing no such thing. We need to go home and let these people eat supper. I'm hankering for some soup."

"See you guys in a while. Don't forget the candy bars, Rosie. You do have some, don't you?"

"Ben, I have a few left. I think they're dark chocolate. Better for you-know-whose health."

"If you need more, I saw some in the convenience store in the office."

"Thank You, Jesus, for Your provisions. Which Larry is limited on."

"Over my dead body."

"You eat the amount you usually do; you'll be ten-toes up before the next tide rolls into the shore."

"And on that happy note, I'm leaving." Larry pretended to hobble away, hunching his shoulders to add to the drama.

"Get going, ya old poop." Rose slapped him on his backside on her way to their trailer. "'Cause the faster we eat, the closer we are to dessert."

"Now you're talking."

CHAPTER FIVE

"Don't make my marshmallows so crispy. If I didn't know better, I'd think your elevated BP is affecting your eyesight."

"It isn't, Rosie, and I make them the same every time."

She made a face behind her husband's back for saying he'd duplicated his earlier masterpieces. He hadn't even come close. Rose rolled the charred remains up in her napkin and made a mental note to toss it in the trash later.

"When Rosie's done daydreaming and figures out what to do with her half-eaten S'more, maybe she'll tell us about the text she got from Jeff and Mary." Larry laid the hanger he'd been using next to the fire pit.

"I almost forgot. Mary said the sale of their property was final on Wednesday. They met with the lawyer and he said everything is done. They can leave whenever they want."

A "Woohoo" and "Praise the Lord" sounded from the other Early Birds around the fire. Rose added a "Yippee Skippy" to the mix then said, "I can't wait to see them again."

"When are they leaving?" Larry picked up the hanger and slid another four marshmallows on the end of it.

"They're heading out the first of next week." Rose glanced over at Larry. "But I'm not sure you're going to live to see them, Larry. You aren't planning on eating all of those, are you?"

"Yes, and please quit worrying about me and my bl—"

"Not worried anymore, dear. You won't be eating them. They're on fire!!!"

Larry threw his hanger into the fire pit. "Guess Someone, other than my wife, is trying to tell me something."

Ben threw his hanger into the fire too. "I'm with you, Lar, I hate it when the Lord yanks my chain about food. How about we get off that topic and talk about who we can help out while we're here?"

"Better subject and it doesn't add inches to my waistline," Rose added with a snort.

"Unless we start making sandwiches again. I brought a good ten pounds back with me from Colorado."

"Ladies, can we let Ben talk? What is the scoop on the church down here?"

"Sounds like it's twofold. For us, they've got a building project going on. Tim said the church here in Mississippi needed some extra hands with all sorts of handyman chores around their new church."

"What's the twofold part?" Rose scooted her chair closer to Ben and the fire.

"This is where you ladies come in. The church runs a daycare for families who need assistance. If the mother doesn't have a job, they help her find one. They work with the women on their resume and find them business clothes to wear."

"Ben, I'm not sure Rose and my ministry is whipping a person's wardrobe into shape for a job interview. We're better with two slices of bread, a jar of jelly, and peanut butter." Betsy smiled. "Anyway, look at us. We're not ready to walk the red carpet in what we're wear—"

"Betsy, hush a moment. I believe our hubbies are challenging us and I beg your pardon, missy, I'm looking good."

"In your dreams."

"Anyway, bring it on, gentlemen, we'll show you how di-ver-si-fied we can be," Rose added extra emphasis on the one word to make her point.

Betsy jumped up and with a sweeping motion and said, "Yes, Rosie, we'll gussy up the women and their resumes. On the way out the door we'll give them a boxed lunch for their first day on the job. We'll show everyone we're di-ver-si-fied."

All form of communication about clothing, S'mores or building a church stalled. The campfire became a comedy club and the four had to quiet each other when stares from the other campers became too numerous.

When things died down Ben spoke up. "Not sure di-ver-si-fied is what I'd call you two, but it sounds like you're ready to broaden your horizons. Tomorrow I'll call the church and see what we can do for them while we're here in Mississippi?"

"How about we get together in the morning, Bets. I'll get on Google and find some second-hand stores we can visit tomorrow. The church has probably got a few lined up, but it doesn't hurt to find others if they don't."

"Noble of you, Rosie. I'm thinking you're looking for an excuse to visit one."

"Is there's a problem with that? You're coming, aren't you?"

"Wouldn't miss it, and all kidding aside, this sounds like fun. Another plus, you guys won't be up to your eyeballs in mud this time."

"If there's drywall to do, we'll be up to our elbows in a different kind of mud."

"Ben, you are becoming so quick witted, but I'm still waiting to hear the joke you started earlier. You know, the one about an architect and engineer walking in somewhere."

"Rosie, I'm not sure what your hubby is talking about, but when I get ready in the morning, I'll come over to your place. See what stores you've found."

Rose hugged her friends and on her way up the steps she watched Ben. She laughed when she caught him nibbling on a couple of marshmallows he'd lightly roasted as the embers died out in the fire pit.

What would they do without their friends. She knew one thing, they'd be old and bored and withering away in The Woodlands, Texas without them. Ben and Betsy made RVing fun again. And whatever happened with Larry's blood pressure, they'd be there to help too.

*Friends. Gotta love 'em.*

"Rose, are you going to shut the door sometime tonight? Give me your phone, I'm sure it needs to go on the charger if you're going to be Googling half the night."

*Yes, friends and a husband I love with all my heart.*

"Lar, I'm right behind you."

"Since it's Thursday night, I'm going to the bedroom to watch the last of the football game. The Saints are playing. While in Biloxi, we root for the home team. However bad they're doing."

"Don't say that too loud. The other campers might tell you a thing or two. Didn't you see our neighbor's flags flapping in the breeze when we parked?"

"Can't say that I did."

"I think it's a great idea. We could buy banners for all the professional teams we root for."

"Why?"

Rose ignored her husband's comment and calculated the flags they needed. "For Ben and you, we'll get the Texans and Astros. Bets must have her Colorado Rockies and Broncos. Me—Kansas City Royals and Chiefs. See that's not too many." She sat down.

"We'll have six flags flying. No, no and no."

"Guess that is a few too many flags flying in one spot. Oh, I forget. Seven with the New Orleans Saints."

"As I said before. No way!"

"Okay, Mr. Absolutely Not. And, just so you know, you're missing your *new,* favorite team. The game is almost over."

"Come on, Baby, I don't know about you, I've heard enough. Next thing that'll happen, Amazon will be delivering a half a dozen flags to my doorstep. Lord, help me."

Rose chuckled as she watched their pooch. Baby bounded over to her dad, barking the whole time. In the process of passing Larry on the steps, the little mutt almost tripped him. Thankfully he grabbed a hold of the rail in time to not take a tumble.

"That little monster is going to kill me one of these days. We should have listened to the vet years ago. 'Teach them how you want them to behave when you're older.' Makes perfect sense now."

"If we'd only listened." Rose giggled as she kicked off her tennis shoes and settled in. Her Google search for second-hand stores showed her three different places. One in particular caught her eye. Sassy Seconds.

"Cute name."

She clicked on the Facebook page and the website took her breath away. Antique fleur de lis designs graced the top of the first page. As she scrolled through the posts, more artistry unfolded before her eyes.

Fashionable pieces of clothing and accessories to fit every woman's needs graced the first page of the website. A couple of clicks later told Rosie she wanted to get acquainted with the resale shop owner. An obvious artist and someone she hoped to do business with.

*Yes, with or without the church.*

"Miss Linda Richeson, you don't know me from Adam, but I believe we're going to get along fine."

"Rosie, you do know she can't hear you. She's in bed. Getting a good night's sleep. Like someone else I know who should be doing the same."

"I'm coming. I'm coming. But you should see this woman's Facebook page and website. WOW!"

"You can show it to me in the morning."

\*\*\*

"See what I told you."

"That is one pretty presentation."

Larry concurred with his wife's assessment. Sassy Seconds would be his choice if he'd ever consider dressing in women's clothing. It'd be the place he'd shop.

"What are you smiling about."

He told Rose what had flashed in his mind about the shop and they had a good chuckle over it.

"I'm sure you'll be sharing this with Ben and Betsy before the day is over."

"Lar, I'll be telling that story until the cows come home and to whoever will listen. You do give me plenty to share with others."

"Glad I can give you material. And speaking of sharing with others. When are you going to tell Ben and Bets about Willie?"

"If the billboards on I-10 haven't already, I thought I'd get her to the store and hopefully find her a pair of boots and tell her then. What do you think?"

"What if they don't carry cowboy boots at the store? This isn't Texas."

"I hadn't thought of that. Thanks for popping my happy

balloon."

"Once again, glad to be of service."

"It'll work out. Somehow. Anyway, I'm not waiting for Bets to come over—I'm going over there right now to share your new clothing propensity."

Rosie walked out of the door, still laughing. Listening to her hoot, hit his funny bone and a few minutes later, while still laughing, Ben came to the door and said, "Sounds like you're enjoying yourself in here. Are you trying on some of Rose's active wear?"

"Doesn't take long for news to travel, does it?"

"Not when it's as good as that little tidbit."

"Don't you have a phone call to make? I'd like to get something accomplished today."

"Larry, you did. You made three, no, make that four people laugh. That's always a great way to start your day. Oh, and reading your Bible."

"Already did that."

"Before or after you tried on Rosie's new hoodie?"

Larry gave his friend a look he hoped would shut him up. It worked, somewhat. Ben still continued to chuckle as he took his phone out and punched in some numbers. He settled down as he spoke into the phone.

Ben then said, "Steve, let me put you on speaker. My partner in crime, Larry Wilford, needs to hear this."

"Hi, Larry. As I was telling Ben, we're right in the middle of our building project. The church is still meeting in the smaller sanctuary, but we're praying we can get in the new building in time for Thanksgiving."

"Pretty tall order with only a month to go."

The minute the words left Larry's lips he wanted to hit himself upside the head. The pastor seemed unfazed when he countered with, "It does seem impossible, but we've seen the Lord work miracles before."

"We have too, and if you don't mind I'd like to start this conversation over. Instead of saying it can't be done, how about we come over today and see how we can help get it accomplished."

"That works. How about 11:00? You can meet the crew of

fifteen volunteers who are coming in from New Orleans."

"See you then. How about we bring lunch?"

"I like you two already."

Larry buttered bread until he thought his arms would fall off. All the while, he prayed for the people they'd have lunch with. Ben took the slices and made turkey and cheese sandwiches, sliding them into baggies when he finished.

"I'm sure glad they ran a special on turkey the other day. Rose snatched up six pounds. Makes for some good eating."

"The extra prayers we said over the sandwiches, which is a trick our sweeties taught us, these workers won't know what hit them." Ben put the last turkey and cheddar sandwich in the sack and wiped off the counter. "And our wives say we don't listen to them."

"Guess on occasion we do. As I say, praying never hurts a thing."

"Amen."

CHAPTER SIX

"Linda, your shop. It's…incredible."

"Mrs. Wilford, you're too kind."

"Please call her Rose." Betsy piped up. "If you don't, she'll hug you until you do."

"I'm from the South. I understand. I hug everyone. Even if they're dead."

*Even if they're dead?*

Rosie wanted to say something, but anything she thought of seemed inappropriate since they'd only met Linda ten minutes before. But, what fell out of her mouth sounded worse than what had played out in her mind.

"Linda, you're not one of those kind of people who conjures up the spirit world? Those kind who do those say-on-seys."

Rose watched Betsy's mouth fly open and thought if her friend didn't close it soon, one of those palmetto bugs might fly into the hanger. Linda, on the other hand, stood there with a grin playing on her lips and then a full-blown giggle followed.

When Linda got herself under control she said, "Lord have mercy on my soul, Rose. I'm a Bible believing, Southern fried chicken and mashed potatoes kind of girl. No 'say-on-seys' going on here or in my county, if I can help it.

"What I meant about hugging 'dead' people. Those are the

ones who aren't filled with the Holy Spirit quite yet."

"You go, girl. And, I'm so glad you clarified it. I almost ran out of those pretty double doors over there when I thought you communed with the man down under." Rose pointed in the direction of her feet.

"Rosie, may I interrupt your babbling?"

"If you see the need."

"I see a *need*...to get you off the subject of spirits and to tell Linda why we're bothering her at 10:00 in the morning." Betsy walked over and sat down at a white metal table next to the window.

Linda came over and joined Betsy. "Now I'm curious. Why are you two here?"

Rose seated herself and searched for the right words to begin the conversation about the store owner helping them out. If need be. Again, words tumbled out before she stopped them, "Linda, we're on a mission from God. Or, at least I think we are."

"Truth is we've come to ask if you'd like to help out a church here in town. Their Women's Ministry wants to clothe single moms and/or women who can't afford nicer clothes to go on job interviews."

"Since we're full-time RVers, we feel it's our ministry to help wherever we park our rigs." Rose shared some of their adventures in Colorado, hoping Linda would see she hadn't let kooks in her store.

She continued, "Linda, the church we attended in Colorado gave our husbands the name of a church here in Biloxi. We wanted to get involved and help while we're here."

"That's us in a nutshell," Betsy added.

"What's the name of the church?"

Rose suspected Betsy's expression returned to catching flies due to Linda's question. Pretty sure hers matched her friends. At that moment she realized they'd forgotten to find out that important piece of information from their husbands.

*Time to come clean.*

"Funny you should ask that question..." Rose stopped to gather her thoughts.

"Linda, we don't know the answer to your question. We forgot to ask our hubbys," Betsy said.

"In other words, we've put the cart before the horse. The reason being, we wanted to get here to check out your adorable place."

After the laughter died down, Linda said, "I'm not sure a specific church name matters. Whatever is going on sounds like the perfect fit for Sassy Seconds. At this point, if you two are involved, I'm in."

A round of cheers went up around the table. Rose breathed a sigh of relief. Her foot-in-mouth disease hadn't gotten them kicked out of the cutest shop in Biloxi. She couldn't wait to work with Linda Richeson. They'd get along marvelously.

*Is that even a word?*

"Hey, I've got a great idea. Why don't I text Ben to find out the name of the church and the woman in charge of this ministry." Betsy took out her phone and began to type.

"You do that. It's best to get the horse in the right place."

"Huh?"

Rose heard Betsy and Linda's one-word question and saw their quizzical look in her direction. Her attempt to explain usage of an equine brought another round of laughter around the table, but Rose's snorts won out in the end.

When things quieted down again Betsy said, "Linda, Rosie was referring to her earlier statement about us getting the cart before the horse. But what's been coming out of her mouth so far today, I'm not sure."

"Don't judge." Rose winked. "Has Ben texted you back?" Rose changed the subject to get the discussion off of her. No need to scare Linda any more than they already had.

"Ben says for us to contact Jan Kendall at the First Baptist Church. He even sent her phone number."

"Don't need it. Jan and I are best friends. Ever since junior high."

"Kind of like Bets and me."

"However, we've known each other less time. About twelve years. Rosie is much older than me. She grew up in the Midwest during the Dustbowl of the 30s."

This time Betsy's laughter filled the quaint boutique. Rose chuckled at her friend's exaggeration of their age difference of seven years.

*Lord, please send me an appropriate, yet snappy retort.*

Nothing came, so Rose said, "Bets, I have no comeback to your outrageous remark. But I'm sure it's obvious to Linda, and anyone else who sees us together, we're much closer in age. A mere five or six..."

Rose left the last part of the sentence off, hoping Betsy would to. She didn't.

"It's seven, Rosie, but who's counting." Betsy reached over and hugged Rose. "Linda, we are the best of friends and I can't wait to meet yours. How about we get in touch with Jan right now?"

Linda snatched her phone off the table and called, which gave Rosie time to glance around the fanciful shop. The store owner had filled every nook and cranny with gently used pants, blouses, skirts and so much more.

Each article of clothing hung in its own rainbow of color, making for a vibrant display for all to enjoy. The racks urged buyers to search for hidden treasures. But the display on the far wall took Rose's attention away from the apparel all around her.

The hand-crafted wooden signs in every size blanketed the planked-wood wall. Sayings, poems and Bible verses galore. All done in exquisite calligraphy. Rose couldn't keep quiet for one more second.

"Bets, did you see these?"

"Shush. Linda's still on the phone."

"Sorry."

"I've got two ladies here, wanting to help out. Yes, I know. How about I ask them?"

Linda took the phone away. "Jan wanted to know if you two are busy for lunch? Douglas will be in to work at 11:00. We can meet at the Waffle House around noon and discuss things. How's that sound?"

"I'm in," Rose answered for both of them.

"We'll see you then."

"Ladies, I can't wait for you to meet Jan. She gets things done in both Gulfport and Biloxi. Funny, she'd called and left me a message last week and I hadn't gotten back to her. Rose, this truly is a mission from God."

"Preach it, sista. God is good and He's doing something."

Rose went over and gave Linda a big Texas size hug. She'd said she liked them. "How about we get out of your hair. I'm sure you have things to do. See you at noon. Come on, Bets."

As they headed out the door, Rose thought about the other reason they'd come. Cowboy boots.

"Linda, do you happen to have women's boots. Preferably the boot-scootin type."

For a third time in less than an hour Betsy's mouth shot open. This time it resembled the opening to a tunnel. Before her friend could utter a sound, Linda said, "I've lined the cowboy boots on the rack next to the denim skirts."

Rose grabbed Bets and together they hightailed it over to a display fit for the Queen of Country Music.

"Why are we suddenly so interested in cowboy boots?" Betsy yanked on her arm, trying to pry it from Rose's firm grasp.

"No need to know the reason why, my dear. Sit yourself down and let us pick out the perfect pair for you."

Which she and Linda did in short order, after they found a pair on the bottom shelf in Betsy's size. She tried them on and the red boots with silver studs adorning the side and front fit her…to a tee.

"Perfect. We'll take 'em." Rose took out her wallet.

"They're on the house. Wherever you're going in these boots it is sure to be loads of fun."

"You have no idea."

Rose took the sack and smiled as they walked to her truck. Betsy drilled her for information about the boots all the way there. Rosie kept her mouth shut, not wanting to spoil the surprise.

*Lord, You kept the lion's mouth shut for Daniel. Please do it for me today.*

"Fine. If you're not telling me, guess I better text Ben and tell them about our lunch plans. Don't want him wondering whether we died on our way back from the second-hand store."

"Be sure to thank him for the info and tell him we're hitting the floor running."

"I don't run. Unless it's to get away from you." This time Betsy laughed.

Rose pulled away from Sassy Seconds and as she turned on Jefferson Street she glanced at her friend and said, "Exercise is a four-letter word."

"You never did know how to spell."

"Not like you, my writer/editor friend. How is your book coming? You haven't said anything about it in a while."

"Not written a word since we left Colorado. Writer's block has knocked on my door."

"Block. Socks. With this new adventure we're on, plus what went on in Colorado...they should give you lots of ideas for the book we talked through a month ago."

The second Rosie said the words about her friend's book, she regretted bringing it up. Might remind her about Willie. For whatever reason, her words didn't seem to faze Betsy. Or prompt her to say any more about her book or boots. Bets sat over in her seat, staring out the side window.

"Betsy, I know you're moping over there, but you need to remember you're writing for the Lord. He will give you the words. In due time." Rose smiled about Saturday night and Willie's concert on the horizon.

"You're right, but it's like the faucet has turned off. Not a dribble coming out of there."

"This deal with Jan and Linda, it looks like it'll prime the pump. Helping these ladies will give you plenty to write about. Even if we're only here for a few days."

"Or a few weeks. If the Lord has something else in store. You never know. Mom said Snowbirds don't officially land in Florida until after Christmas."

For some reason, at that moment, the signs Rose had seen at Sassy Seconds came to mind. She'd never seen such workmanship in all of their travels.

"Hello, Rose?"

"I'm here."

"Hope so. You're driving."

"At least the road's not too crowded. I can take up both lanes, if I want to." Rose sneaked a peek at her friend and laughed.

"Please don't."

"I won't and what I was thinking about, if you're still interested, were the signs at Linda's shop. You shushed me about the time I wanted to show them to you."

"What's so special about them?"

"Whoever did the lettering on them has more talent in their

46

pinky toe than I have in my roly-poly body. I wanted to ask Linda about them when she got off the phone."

"You were too busy picking out boots for me."

Rose held her breath, waiting for another round of questions to start coming about the purchase. They never came so she said, "Never mind."

"You can 'Never mind' me all you want, Rosie. Anyway, you will see Linda at lunch. You can ask her about them then."

"If I forget, it'll give us another excuse to visit her store."

"Sometimes, Mrs. Wilford, you're brilliant and someone who's not telling me something."

"Uh huh! Now how about we turn on the GPS and find the Waffle House. I'm starving after perusing all the pretties. I'm peckish."

"Rosie, your alliterations are abnormal."

Before she could reply, the GPS told Rose to turn at the next corner. She followed the directions instead of countering her friend. But after parking, she turned to Bets and said, "Wheeling into the Waffle House made me weary."

"You're getting on my nerves."

"That's my lot in life, little lady."

"That one's a stretch. Stop it now!" Betsy put her hands in the air. "The good thing about this conversation, we're alone. Unlike this morning. It wouldn't surprise me if Linda didn't call Jan and tell her, 'We need to get out while we can. These two are lunatics.'"

"It would be their loss. We're as good as it gets, girlfriend."

"You are officially the winner. I give up."

"That's good. Linda and Jan are here. Didn't chase them off after all."

"At least one of us didn't."

"Always have to have the last word." Rose unbuckled her seatbelt and opened her door to step out. Before she made it out all the way, Betsy appeared on her side of the truck.

"You know it." Bets smiled. "And, Rose, please promise me you'll behave."

"I will if you will."

"Deal."

***

47

Larry knew his wife and Betsy could ramble on for days if he didn't step in to stop the gale force winds coming at them at the table that evening.

"Dear, it sounds like you two had a great morning and afternoon. Can Ben and I get a word in on this too?"

"Sure, but don't talk too long it's almost dinner time."

"Didn't we just eat lunch, Rose?"

"Hon, having experienced lunch with you and your writing group, I'm not sure much eating took place. Too much chatting going on."

Larry gave Ben a high five and said, "Why *do* women go out to eat. I'll never understand. Go get a coffee and let the talking begin."

"Not happening, Lar. I'm not going to Starbucks and have Rosie get tickled after she's taken a drink of her coffee. Me and everyone else, we'd be wearing the proceeds. Personally, I don't want to see coffee dripping out of her nose."

"At least I've never had cheddar cheese collecting dust on my chin while dining at Taco Bell. Unlike someone else we know and love...Betsy."

Rose snorted, which caused their pooch to jump out of her pet bed and bark to high heaven. Matilda, who'd been lying under the table, joined in with a woof or two of her own, finishing her show by chasing Baby around the living room.

"Can't blame them for getting excited at the noise Rosie makes. It startles me at times too."

"With that snide comment, it's your turn to feed Baby."

Larry got up and went behind the counter and opened the cabinet next to the sink. "Are you two hungry? Mats, don't worry, I've got some for you, as well." Another chorus of yelps sounded while Larry filled the dog dishes.

"While I'm up, isn't it our dinnertime too?" Larry grabbed the soup bowls and filled them with chicken soup out of the crockpot. "Hope it tastes as good as it smells."

"Need any help?"

"Nope. Got it under control." He put the soup at each plate and turned to get the crackers and butter and set them on the table.

"You forgot one thing, dear, something to eat it with."

Larry reached over the island and got four spoons and knives

48

out of the drawer. "Now can I sit down?"

He didn't wait for any of them to answer and joined them, handing each their utensils as he sat down. He took his spoon and dipped it into the steaming broth and almost had it to his mouth, when he saw six eyes staring at him.

"You forgot something else, my love."

He swallowed the bite and said, "Can do."

Larry proceeded with a somewhat lengthy prayer and as he was about to close, one of them kicked him.

"In Jesus name. Amen!

"Sorry, dear, you were going on for days. My soup was getting cold."

"Next time you can pray."

"We'd never get to eat if Rosie prayed. Or find out who Steve is. Larry, whoever he is, he's blessed beyond measure with what you said."

"Hon, Steve is the pastor of the church. His situation is similar to Jeff and Mary. In their case, they lost everything in a fire." Ben took a bite of his soup and grimaced. "Sorry, Lar, but your soup needs more salt. Can you hand it to me, Bets?"

Larry ignored his friend's comment and added, "Steve also lost his home in Hurricane Katrina."

"Not trying to be funny, but are you sure his name isn't Job." Betsy dangled the salt shaker in front of Ben. "Do you really need to salt your soup, dear? Can anyone at this table say, 'Elevated blood pressure?'"

"Yes, I'd like some salt, Rosie Too. And as hard as we worked today, I sweat everything out of me. Think I read somewhere that you need to replenish what you lose."

"Don't know for sure, but a little less salt would do us all some good." Betsy took another bite.

"She's right. Now back to Steve. Does he have a family?"

"He does and that's where your culinary skills will come in handy again." Larry put his spoon next to his bowl. "I know they'd appreciate food. I'm sure cooking while you're displaced isn't fun."

Larry heard his friend chuckle and Ben said, "And when you're done doing that, you can help Steve's wife feed the kids at the daycare."

"Why, Lord?" Bets laughed and reached across the table. "Give me the salt. I'm going to pour it down my throat to hurry my journey to heaven. Cooking in a daycare. Life on earth is too hard."

"I've heard more dramatic tales today, but that one tops them all."

Betsy raised her head off the table. "Thanks, Larry, and all kidding aside, you can count on me to help Steve and his family. And just so you guys know, we had a saga of our own at Sassy Seconds, but I'll let Rosie fill you in on it."

"I can't wait to hear what she has to say."

They listened to Rose, and on occasion Betsy popped in with a snippet about their day. Larry wondered how two women made friends so fast.

"I know I said I'd let Rosie tell you, but I have to say—in both of our defenses—when we get going we forget we're with other people. I'm sure Linda is still talking about the two of us."

"I'm sorry to say it all started when I asked the store owner a simple question."

"Whether she tried to call up dead people." Betsy took a cracker off Rose's plate.

"Leave my food alone and it wasn't like that at all."

"One of you please explain why my wife even went down that road in the first place." Larry almost wanted to cover his ears to keep from hearing what Rose said.

"Linda said she hugs the dead."

Larry and Ben burst out laughing. At one point it got so bad Rosie got up to get a box of Kleenex, handing out tissues to everyone. Larry wiped his eyes and asked, "I'm pretty sure she meant something else."

"She did," Betsy said. "After I mentioned that Rose is a hugger, Linda said she hugs everyone. Even the dead."

"And that's when I asked if she did say-on-seys."

"Rosie, you do say the darndest things." Ben took a cracker off of Larry's plate this time.

"Do you mind? I wanted that one."

"Anyway, Linda cleared up the 'dead' comment. She's like me, she likes to grab non-believers and squeezes them until nothing's left then the Holy Spirit can march on in and take up residence."

Again the table erupted into fits of laughter. Larry wanted to comment on what Rose had said, but anytime he tried, he'd laugh even harder. Oh how he adored his loveable, yet quirky wife and her ability to bring the house down and not even know why.

When order came to the Wilford's dining room, Betsy added, "Still think Linda thought the Looney Tunes visited her today."

"After the lunch we had with Jan and Linda, we ALL fit into the nuttier than normal category."

"How about we get off that subject? What are you two going to be doing?" Ben reached over and took more crackers out of the package and buttered them.

"Before we get to that," Betsy laid her spoon down. "I need to ask Larry something."

He watched. Her eyes never blinked or wavered from his. Larry knew she wanted information and he wasn't about to divulge anything about the concert. To stay out of the middle of his wife's shenanigans he answered, "I know nothing. You need to ask Rosebud."

"I haven't even asked the question."

"My answer is the same."

"Can someone tell me the question? I'm dying to know."

"Ben, I'm now the proud owner of a pair of cowboy boots. All I'm trying to find out is why I suddenly need them."

"Tomorrow's another day, so let's say we drop this boot bonanza for now and talk about it in the morning." Rosie smiled and buttered one of the crackers off Ben's plate. "Here sweetie, fill your mouth with this. Then you won't be able to ask any more questions."

"As I said before—you're up to something and I'm not sure I like it."

"Oh, you'll love this one. Now back to Ben's earlier question. What was it again?"

"What will you two be doing at the church?"

"We're making sure each woman who signs up for the program is taken care of. I'm excited to help them find the perfect outfit for their job interviews. It'll be like we're playing dress up."

"And while we're finding them something to dress up in from Sassy Seconds, Jan and two other ladies from the church will work with them on their resumes. I'm with Rosie, I can't wait to get going."

Larry moved over to the couch and enjoyed watching Betsy and his wife. Their new lifestyle of helping people agreed with Rose. Sad it took them into their mid-to-late 60s to reach out and bless others.

*Thank You, Lord, for getting through to this old geezer's heart.*

CHAPTER SEVEN

"You did what?"

"I bought the VIP tickets to Willie's concert."

Rose suspected her hubby wanted to run and check online banking, but he stayed put for one reason: he couldn't remember his password.

"How much? Forget it. I don't want to know."

"Let's just say tonight's foray will cover us from ever having to buy the Stevenson's a gift for the rest of our lives."

"Since I didn't get a say in this, I'll be the one standing on the street corner selling my ticket. Trying to recoup some of the monies you spent."

"I think not. You'll be the one videotaping us meeting Willie."

"Willie who?"

Voices she recognized came from outside. Instead of letting their uninvited guests in, she turned to Larry and said, "Sweetums, the next time you go outside in the morning, don't leave the door wide open."

"Why, Rosie?" Betsy questioned as she walked into the Wilford's RV. "Are you worried they'll hear something they're not supposed to?"

Ben stepped inside and said, "I heard Willie and tickets in the same sentence. What's going on?"

Unable to get out of the inevitable, Rose shouted at the top of her lungs, "Strap on your cowboy boots and hat. We're all going to see Willie (On The Road Again) Nelson in concert tonight at the Mississippi Moon."

Rosie didn't realize a grown woman could shriek off key, but Betsy did it. Her friend jumped around as if her tail feathers had caught fire and she wanted to find a place to put them out. This reaction came without her knowing they had top-of-the-line seats.

"Girl, I'm not sure our RV will withstand the impact of the other bit of news I need to tell you, so why don't we sit on the couch. I'll hold you down and Larry will fill you in on the next big news."

Rose made her usual noise as she ushered Bets over to the couch and they sat down. To make sure she curbed her friend's enthusiasm, she threw her leg over Betsy's and told her hubby, "Hit it."

"Bets, she bought the really expensive tickets to the concert, so you'd be front and center to see Willie."

"How much?" Ben asked.

"Do men always need to know the price? There's no need for specifics. They're bought and paid for. All we need to do is show up and enjoy the concert."

Betsy gave Rose a hug and said, "I can't believe you got us tickets to see Willie."

"I can't either." Ben and Larry said at the same time."

"The two of you need to hush up. This'll be a kick in the pants."

"And, thanks to Rosie, I'll be sporting my new *red* cowboy boots." Betsy stood and dangled her leg out in front of her as if she showed them her new attire. "Oh, I got so excited, I forgot I don't have them on yet."

"Bets, the boots almost blew the lid off the whole deal. Girl, you ask too many questions."

"Long before the boots, I knew you were hiding something from me. I can read you like a book."

"Which is why I bought the tickets. If you're going to write a novel, you need inspiration to ward off the writer's block. What better way to get inspired than to see the man behind the idea for it?"

"And Rosie thinks Willie needs to know that you're writing a book. You'll tell him when you see him backstage."

"Larry?" Rose ran to their bedroom and slammed the door.

"Oops."

"Ben, it's time for us to leave. Lar, you can call us with the specifics later."

"I don't think we're leaving until 5:00 or 5:30, but I'll let you know."

*\*\**

"Larry Wilford, ice cream will not get you out of the dog house any sooner."

"Can't fault a man for trying."

"You're trying. That's for sure." Rose put the last spoonful of Rocky Road in her mouth and slipped on her blue jeans and tucked in the still-hot-from-the-iron Western shirt. To top off her ensemble, she tied a bright blue bandana around her neck.

She'd put on her pink boots when she sat on the couch. No need to cram her feet into the pointy toes until they took off. Rose glanced at the wall. 4:55. Almost time to leave. Only thing they needed – tickets, a prayer she'd get them noticed and backstage, and a new husband.

Two out of the three would win the day, but at the moment she wanted to cut Larry's leg off at the knee and beat him with it for telling Betsy her plan.

Or-lack-thereof plan.

She did wonder how she'd get them backstage to meet the legend. Would an old woman flailing her arms get his attention? Probably not.

*Think Rosie. Think.*

She had it. She'd faint dead away…not really out…out, but they'd come running to give her aid. She wouldn't tell the men, but fill Betsy in on the specifics. "When I'm down, run to the side of the stage. They're sure to bring me in that direction."

"Rosie, are you talking on the phone? We need to get going pretty soon."

"Ready when you are."

She picked up Baby and whispered, "I don't know what I'm going to do, but whatever it is—it'll be a doozer, I'm sure."

Then it hit her. She slipped on her cowboy boots and waltzed over to the kitchen counter where she'd left a pad of paper. Rosie scribbled a quick note and stuffed it into her back pocket. "Yes, my work here is done...almost."

"Anyone home in there?"

Rose came around the island and opened their screen and said, "Well, aren't we snazzy? I'm loving those boots, Bets."

"Me too."

"You got the tickets?" Larry moved past her and went down the stairs.

"Right in here in my fanny pack. We're on the road again."

Rose heard the groans, but ignored her friends as they got in the Wilford's truck. When she settled in, she got out the parking pass and said, "Larry, you'll need this. Put it on the mirror. Sounds like all we do is follow the signs for VIPs."

"Oh la la. Doesn't that make you feel like a queen, Rosie?"

"No more than the fact that we're daughters of the King of kings, and we're His bride...guess that does make us Queens."

"Rosie, only you'd make a biblical story out of going to a Willie Nelson concert."

"You know it."

***

"Front row seats?"

"Can you believe it? And center stage, too. Bets, if this doesn't put a fire under your behind to write—nothing will. Now if you'll excuse me, I need to use the ladies room."

"I better go, too." Betsy walked toward the aisle.

"No, let me...find it. I'll come back...and..."

"And I can come right now and we'll find it together."

"Rose, what are you doing?"

"Nothing, Larry. I'm sure Betsy's toes are as pinched as mine and I wanted to save her some steps."

"Sure you did." Betsy sat down. "Go ahead. I'm too excited to worry about your wackier than normal behavior."

As Rose hurried away, she glanced at her watch. Fifteen minutes to put her plan into action and get back to her seat. If everything worked the way she hoped, she'd get in a potty break, which would come in handy.

Rosie eyed the two men standing at the side door of the stage. What could it hurt if she went and chatted with them? If they didn't want anything to do with her, they'd tell her to go back to her assigned seat.

Or, call for security when she broached the subject of wanting a back-stage pass. She could hear them. "Ma'am, we've been waiting all night to let you in here. No worries that you've been lurking around here, staring us down. Sure, come on back. Willie always likes to start his concert out wondering if someone's going to go bonkers on him. NOT! Take her away, officer."

Rosie shook her head and recited the first verse she thought of, "...*in God I trust; I will not be afraid. What can mortal man do to me?*"

She chuckled at her choice of Bible verses and couldn't be certain if that wasn't the strangest passage she'd ever come up with in her time of need. And from the look on the security guard's face—she must have said it out loud. He came over and asked, "May I help you?"

"You sure can, young man. I need to find a way to get backstage." Rose reached into her back pocket and retrieved the piece of paper she'd put there earlier. "Can you give this note to Mr. Nelson? It's of utmost importance he sees it before the concert starts."

"Strict rules, ma'am. No concert goer gets back-stage access. Ever. Now find your seat."

Rose's face flush and the wardrobe choice she'd made earlier, i.e. blue bandana around her neck, held all the heat in check. She knew if she didn't let off some steam, the top of her head would explode and leave an awful mess for them to clean up.

"Ma'am, are you alright?"

"No, I'm not. I spent an insane amount of monies to get in here. Five-hundred smackers to be exact. That amount should get me and my friend something. At this point we'd settle for a peek around the corner at Willie. Maybe even a "howdy do, sir" as he walked out on stage."

"Please find your seat. The concert is almost ready to start."

Rose could tell the man wanted nothing more to do with her. As she turned to leave she said, "Please give him this note. Tell him it's from Rose and Betsy. We're in the front row. Thanks."

"Can't promise you anything."

Rosie found her seat and the lights flickered. When the

opening act came on stage the concert goers stood to their feet and cheered. Larry took ahold of her hand and squeezed it. She wanted to tell him she'd failed, but decided to leave it alone and see if the Lord had anything up the sleeve of His robe.

This image caused Rose to chuckle, which led to more racket coming out of her. Thankfully the noise at the Mississippi Moon drowned out any commotion she caused. The rest of the Early Birds stood clapping, never having a clue she entertained herself.

Grapevine Express played for thirty-five minutes. The younger people in the crowd knew every one of their songs. Some old and one or two rap/country tunes finished off their set. Lots of cheering sent them off the stage.

They returned, and the band's last song, *God Bless the U.S.A.,* prompted everyone to stand and turn the flashlights on their phone. As the lights dimmed in the auditorium, thousands of voices raised to sing along.

*What a great way to end. Thank You, Lord.*

After they left the stage, Rose made a break for the side door. She'd rounded the corner when she felt a pull on the back of her shirt and Betsy asked, "Going somewhere?"

"Ladies room. Want to come?"

"If we're going in the same stall? You're not getting out of my sight."

"That's not happening." Rose slipped in one and locked the door.

When they came out and stood at the sink, Rose caught Betsy gawking at her in the mirror.

"What?"

"What are you up to?"

"Nothing."

"Nothing, my foot. Tell me what you've done."

She told her friend from start to finish and Betsy's eyes grew wider and wider until Rose said, "Better close 'em or they're going to pop clean out of their sockets."

"I cannot believe...oh, who am I kidding? Why wouldn't I think you're capable of almost anything to get us backstage."

"Stay tuned, it's about to get more interesting."

"No, it isn't. We're going back to our seats. Right now."

"You mean I can't faint by the security guy? It'd work.

They'd have to sweep me up fast so the show could go on."

"They'd do something with you. But we're going back to our seats so they don't need to figure out what to do with you."

"You're no fun."

"You'll thank me in the morning.

"I doubt it."

Rose and Betsy made it to their seats right when they announced the main event. "Give Willie Nelson a Mississippi welcome."

The audience jumped to their feet as he strolled out on the stage singing, *Good Hearted Woman.*

Rose looked around and everyone knew the Waylon and Willie song, including her. She wondered when she'd listened to it long enough to learn it, but put her thoughts to rest and enjoyed the song.

His next selection, *Beer for My Horses,* Rosie had never heard before. No one in their group seemed to know the words either. Someone, in the middle of the catchy tune, leaned over and told her it'd been a hit for Willie and Toby Keith.

*Who knew? Not me.*

Willie entertained the sold-out crowd with all of his hits. One right after another. While he sang, Rose made as much noise as she could to get noticed. And, short of standing on her fold down padded seat, she'd pass. No need to kill herself for the cause.

But fainting still shouted to her as an option and when Willie walked to the edge of the stage, Rose couldn't be sure if Betsy and her wouldn't take turns on who landed on who.

"Hello, ladies."

Rose glanced over at Betsy and the two pointed at the other and said, "Us?"

"Yes, I have a note here from Rose, which of you is her?"

"Me."

"I'm telling you, if everybody had a friend like you, this world would be a better place to live in."

Rose pinched her arm, making sure she hadn't passed out after all.

*No, this is really happening. Oh my. Oh my. Oh my.*

"Rose and Betsy, I'd like you to join me on stage. Together, we're going to sing *On the Road Again.*"

The women hopped up and rushed to the stairs. On their way up, 'Guido' gave Rose a piece a paper. She gave him a questioning look, but he pushed them forward. Betsy grabbed her hand and the two went to stand next to Willie Nelson.

*Oh my goodness.*

While strumming his guitar he asked, "What key would you like to sing the song in?"

"You pick. We stink at singing."

Laughter rang out and Rose couldn't believe her friend had spoken up so boldly. She'd remind her later that she hadn't died when she spoke in front of people. Even if it only encompassed six words.

Willie pointed to a monitor for them to follow along on his signature song. He began and everyone joined in. Who knew the first time the two friends sang karaoke, they'd be doing it on stage with Willie Nelson.

The song finished and Willie hugged them and said, "Thank you for making my evening a little more special."

They exited the stage and Rose decided if she died at that moment, she'd die happy. She'd bought the ticket for Betsy, but she'd come out a HUGE fan of the superstar. Rosie sat down and opened the paper the young man gave her.

"After the concert, come to the stairs. Y'all are going backstage."

***

The music to *On the Road Again* played as Willie exited the stage. Betsy's smile warmed Rosie's heart and no matter the cost—the evening topped anything she'd witnessed in her 60-plus years.

*And there's more to come. Some hobnobbing.*

When their path to the stairs cleared, Rosie instructed the other Early Birds to follow her to the stage. However, in giving directions with her one arm flapping in the air, she hit something.

Rose spun around to see what she'd come in contact with. A man stood behind her with his spectacles hanging precariously off one of his ears.

"Oh, sir, I'm so sorry."

"Not a problem, lil' lady. I'm glad your aim wasn't any higher. Might have sent my Stetson flying clean across the hall."

The cowboy righted his glasses, tipped his hat, and moved away.

"You have a good day too."

"Hon, let's get going before you bloody someone's nose next time."

Larry took her arm and the four of them made it over to the stairway. One of the men she'd spoken to earlier motioned for them to come up.

"I can't believe this is happening."

"Betsy, make us proud."

"Doing what?"

"Doing whatever writers do."

"We write."

Rosie wanted to laugh at Betsy's comment, but thought better of it. Didn't want to scare Willie with one of her snorts.

The entertainer sat on the couch, talking with three people, when they came in the room. The minute he saw them he told the others, "I'll talk about this later. Now I have a more important meeting."

For the next ten minutes, Rose and Betsy became the star's focus. Ben and Larry stood on the sideline. Neither saying a word.

"So, Rose, tell me about this note?"

Before she could answer, Betsy jumped in. "Sir, I'm not sure what she wrote you, but I'm sure it's pure foolishness, knowing my friend."

"Was not."

"Was too."

Willie slapped his knee and said, "I am so glad I had the privilege of meeting you two. Why don't you take turns and tell me what's going on and what my song has to do with it?"

Betsy went first and shared the importance of his song. "Mr. Nelson, my idea is to write a novel, loosely based on the four of us RVing. Your song *On the Road Again* is Ben and my song whenever we hit the road. Now, with Larry and Rose the 'best friends' line is icing on the cake."

"She's telling you the truth, Mr. Nelson. We're singing your song, ever so poorly, as we go down the highways and byways. Can't think of a better idea for a novel."

"I love the idea and the song, of course, but please call me Willie," He winked then said, "Betsy, be sure to send me a copy when you get published. I want to read it."

"Will do. Now we better go. We've taken too much of your time." Betsy stood and swooned.

Rose hurried to her side to steady her and said, "Yes, we have. Need to get out of your hair."

"Ladies, it's been a pleasure. Come back anytime. Backstage is always open." He hugged Rose and Betsy again and shook the men's hand.

Rose wiped a tear from her eye as they exited and she couldn't help but smile at everything. From start to finish.

*Yes, Lord, a dream come true. You orchestrated quite a special evening for all of us.*

CHAPTER EIGHT

Sunday morning, after the big concert, Rose climbed out of bed and announced, "We're going to church, but the rest of the day – I'm relaxing. My head's still thumping from the noise from last night."

"How about we make a lunch for all of us and take it over to the beach?"

"Mr. Wilford, has anyone told you that you're brilliant?"

"Not so far today."

"Then I guess it's official and it's time to go to church." Rose grabbed her purse and opened the door. "Baby, we'll be back in a little bit. You be good."

They made early service, but the rest of the day, after making their picnic lunch, they sat in their lawn chairs and vegged at the beach. The gentle ocean breeze and the warm sand under Rose's feet lulled her to sleep.

Until laughter woke her from a dead sleep. She straightened in her chair and her husband and two friends watched her. Rose noticed that Betsy put her phone down and another round of giggles broke out.

"Let me see your phone."

"There's nothing to see." Betsy closed her eyes and leaned back in her chair. She then tilted her head from one side to the other. "Nope. Not a thing to see."

"Give me your phone. I'll determine whether that's a true statement, or not."

"Lar, she does wake up cranky, doesn't she?"

"Sometimes."

Ben swung his legs around on his chaise lounge and said, "After her carrying on at the concert last night, I'd be worn out too."

"I am, but don't get off the subject. Hand it over, sister. Or I'll come over and sit on you."

"The chair won't hold both of us."

"That's the truest statement you've said in the last five minutes." Rose got up from her chair and walked the few feet to stand in front of Betsy and put her hand out.

"Oh alright."

Rosie hit Gallery and listened to the video her friend took of her. The saving grace to the footage—no one heard her snoring over the wind gusts. Funny how the bursts of laughter came through though. Loud and clear.

She shut off the noise and placed the phone on the arm of Betsy's chair. Then she waltzed to her own and in one quick movement, she folded up her lawn chair and set it down at the water's edge.

Rosie then took on the stance she'd witnessed in the video and said, "Go ahead. Post it on Facebook, but be sure to tell everyone the reason why I'm pooped. I have three other people I must keep entertained at all times."

"And you do an excellent job, Rosebud. Are we ready to go back to the RVs? We've got a busy week, starting tomorrow."

***

Monday morning arrived and the four of them made it to the church to begin volunteering. Rose registered the young ladies and Betsy took them to Sassy Seconds to pick out two outfits to wear on their interviews.

Rosie busied herself around the church, helping wherever they needed her. At 3:30, Betsy brought the last lady back to the church. They gathered in the basement and Rose gushed when Kate modeled her clothing.

"Dear, I cannot get over how pretty you look."

Bets buttoned the sleeve on the young woman's jacket and stepped back. "Parakeet blue is your color."

"Parakeet blue?"

"My mom sewed for me when I was growing up. It's the color she used for almost all of my outfits that one year. I've never forgotten it."

"You sound like my dad." Kate glanced at them in the three-way mirror. "He remembers the color of their first car. I can't believe it still sticks with me. It was Gunmetal Gray."

"Memories are precious, hon." Rose finished ironing a shell she'd found and gave it to Kate. "Here you go. Hurry now. I can't wait to see you in this next number."

"I feel like I'm on the show *What Not to Wear.*" Kate laughed as she slipped inside one of the children's Sunday school rooms, carrying the freshly ironed shell.

"Rosie, I don't know about you, but I'm having an absolute blast. Kate is stunning. Have you ever seen longer lashes? Mine would win the Stumpy Award."

"I agree. I mean about Kate's lashes." Rose snorted.

"Glad you cleared up the confusion."

Rose wanted to give her friend a little bit more trouble, but kept quiet and tidied the room. No need to harass the help. They'd drawn the straws, fair and square, as to who'd stay at the church or who'd go to the shop the first day.

She'd drawn the short one. Obviously the Lord hadn't heard her prayers, begging for Him to send her first. But, not to worry, tomorrow she'd get her opportunity to work her razzmatazz on the next special woman.

"Rosie, are you still stewing about the Lord shining His great blessing on me?"

"No and the only thing the Savior is illuminating in you is…is…" Rose heard a door slam and she turned around to see Kate coming down the hall toward them. "Oh goodness sakes." Her voice caught in her throat.

When Rose did try to speak, only a squeak came out. After swallowing she said, "Lord, You've outdone Yourself this time. Kate, the way that skirt fits you, it could stop a freight train dead on its tracks."

"Ditto to what she said."

"Thank you." Kate blushed and fiddled with the hem of her jacket.

"You're more than welcome. Please let us know how your job interview goes."

"I will." Kate peered down at her wrist. "Better change and get going. Got a class in thirty minutes."

"Here's a bag for you to put all your clothes in."

"Thanks again."

After Kate left, Rose and Betsy walked back to the church's foyer to search for Jan, but found Linda instead, sitting on the piano bench.

"Hello, ladies."

"Hi to you too."

Linda stood and pulled an item out of the sack she carried. "I know I've already given Kate two outfits, but I found one more thing for her. It'll be perfect, and it has nothing to do with work clothes."

Rose almost danced over to see what Linda brought with her, but slowed her steps when her companion lagged behind her.

"Am I the only one excited here? Could you speed it up?"

Instead of hurrying, Betsy slowed her steps even more. To make matters worse, Linda joined the party in the vestibule. She dropped the bag on the stool and the two of them carried on for a good minute.

At that moment Rosie knew how her hubby felt when his blood pressure hit the roof and said as much, "I'd like to say I'm finding your slow-poke antics funny, but I'm not. You two need to stop your nonsense this very minute." Not to appear too feisty, Rose added a smile.

The store owner and Bets settled down enough for Linda to open the bag and drape a leather coat over her arm. The light from the floor-to-ceiling windows hit its varied colors of cream, taupe and shades of brown.

Rose gasped. Kind of. More like a miniature snort. She'd never set eyes on a more beautiful item. If this had fit over her larger-than-life backside, she'd have paid Linda a large sum to make it her own.

But she knew no part of the size six stunner fit her. Not by a long shot. She'd hold out hope for heaven. Forget the here and now.

"Linda, we've lost her. Rosie's got that far off look in her eyes and she won't be worth living with when she tells me about it later."

"Tell you what? I'm okeedokie."

"Sure you are. Anyway, I can't wait to see Kate when she sets her eyes on this." Betsy ran her fingers over the leather and said, "We'll have to wait until tomorrow. Kate left before we found you out here."

"Linda, she is going to flip when she sees it."

"I hope so. Gotta run." Linda grabbed her purse and a flurry of hugs commenced before any of them got out the door.

After the final hug Rose said, "We better scoot, too. I'm sure Bets will want to share with me her expertise at picking out clothing for the ladies. By the way, what is the woman's name I'm helping tomorrow?"

"Everly. Like the—"

"Everly Brothers."

"Rose, I don't think she's any relation to them."

"*Bye, Bye Love.* My all-time favorite song of theirs. Which is what we need to do. Bye, Bye, Linda. See ya in the morning."

Rose dropped off the jacket in one of the rooms they'd used and went to her truck. Her cohort, however, stood chatting with Linda. Perhaps the best place for her since Rosie's mood took a nose dive. And a gorgeous jacket had sent her there on the express train.

She grasped the fact she'd never measure more than five foot and some change, but one time, a long, long, long time ago Larry told her, "You need to put some meat on those bones." She'd complied. Over and above what the charts at the doctor's office said she should weigh.

They suggested between 107 to 141 due to her short stature. "Which means at my weight, I should measure well over six foot seven inches."

"Six foot seven. No, Kate isn't that tall."

"I wasn't talking about her." Rose peered over at Betsy as she got in the truck. "I calculated it in my head. That's the height I need to be for how much I weigh. Ever calculated what your height should be?"

"Thanks for telling me I'm rotund."

"I didn't."

"Did too."

"Okay, maybe I did. Sorry. Guess I wanted someone to join the pity party I'm having. As you know, partying is no fun without company."

"I wondered what was going on with you. But may I digress a moment before I hop into your par-tay? Back to the weight charts? Don't pay any attention to them." Betsy fastened her seat belt.

After Rose pulled out of the parking lot and headed to the RV Park she asked, "You don't?"

"Nope. No need to. Jesus Loves Me."

"Yes, He does. And, so you know, you got some extra points on that one, Bets."

"Hope so. I need all I can get."

Rose did feel the tension in her neck and back relax. She hadn't realized the coat had affected her so much. But her friend's simple reminder made her take a deep breath and made her realize she'd taken her eyes off the only thing that mattered. The Lord.

"Rosie, you never did tell me the reason for your pity party? Why's your weight bothering you all of a sudden?"

"The jacket Linda showed us. Seeing it chapped my hide. No pun intended."

Rose heard laughter coming from the passenger's side, but she had to stay focused as she parked next to Ben and Betsy's dually. When she put the truck in Park and shut it off, she got tickled and joined in the more joyous party. This made for a much better end to her day.

Betsy took her seatbelt off and leaned toward her and said, "Rosie, there's another reason for your mood. You consumed way too much sodium nitrates in the soup the other night."

"Thought diagnosing was *my* job." Rose laughed then added, "No, Bets, I'm pretty sure it was the leather jacket from Sassy Seconds. Why didn't the Lord make me taller and not so wide?"

"I'm not answering that on the premise you'll kill me."

"You are wise beyond your years." Rose hopped out of her truck and walked over to Betsy to give her a hug. "Tomorrow, will you remind me to ask Linda about those calligraphy signs in her shop. I keep forgetting."

"You don't have wall space in your RV for one of them."

"Who said I was only buying one?"

"Rosie, we're on a budget." Larry stuck his head out their front door.

"Hi, hon. Thanks for the reminder. Bets, I'll see you in the morning. Don't forget to call your mom. She's probably wondering if we're ever leaving Mississippi."

"The call to your mom will have to wait, Betsy." Larry came down the stairs. "We invited some of our neighbors for dinner."

"Brats, hotdogs and S'mores anyone?" Ben came out of the Stevenson's RV, carrying a tray of meat."

"You feeding an army? After the conversation Betsy and I had coming home, I'm not sure I'm hungry."

"Jesus loves you."

"He does, doesn't He. Well, let's get those dogs cooking."

While Larry brought the buns and condiments out and put them on the table, the couple from the RV next door came over. The man's name escaped him, even though he'd heard it less than an hour before when he'd taken Ben and him inside of his Class C when they got home from working at the church.

After the tour and when they sat outside, Ben suggested they invite their neighbors to a cookout. "Bet's made a batch of her potato salad last night. There's enough to go around."

"Wouldn't we rather keep it all for ourselves?" Larry's mouth watered thinking about Betsy's delicious side dish.

"No, Bets and I talked. We've been pretty lax at the other parks. I thought the fun of getting on the road was to meet our fellow campers."

"My idea has always been to spend time with you two and Rose. When I'm not doing that, I stay in the house and—"

"Play games on your iPad."

"Not anymore."

"Lar, there's more out here. Come out and experience it."

"This coming from an ex-workaholic. Okay, Ben, you win this time. I'll work on my social skills."

A visit to the other RV had stretched his socialization as far as he wanted to go, but seeing inside the rig made him realize he liked what he saw. A smaller unit. Only three or four feet larger than their king cab dually truck.

*Rose would be able to drive it.*

"Are you going to put the meat on the grill today, Mr. Wilford? Or is the conversation in your head more interesting?"

"You should know all about that, my dear."

Larry chuckled while he distributed the meat on the propane fire pit/grill. Once they started to sizzle, he turned to the man who owned the smaller unit and asked, "I'm sorry, what is your name again?"

"John and Shirley Lawton and the two coming up the driveway are Dwayne and Nicole James."

"Thanks. Get settled in and it won't be long before the meat's ready."

Larry glanced at the table on his way inside the RV and realized he'd forgotten to grab the chips and utensil holder thingamajig. He gave the items to Rose when they headed back out the door.

He followed her down the stairs to check on the hotdogs and brats and while he stood there—he carried on a conversation with the other men. Looking in his wife's direction, Rosie sat and chatted with the women like she'd known them all her life.

Truth be told Rosebud could talk to a light pole and get mad at it if it didn't answer back. Unlike him. He'd rather hit them. Larry laughed as he turned the fire down and headed over to the picnic table where the group of guys now stood.

Larry must have appeared to Ben like he stood in his underwear among clothed people. His friend hurried over and whispered, "The one to your left is Dwayne. On his right – he's John."

"It helps if you associate the names to someone you know. I find it much easier." John Lawton came up and got a water out of the cooler.

"I'll try it. Thanks."

*And while I'm at it, I'll master small talk with total strangers.*

Then a grand idea hit Larry. He walked up to John and asked, "Is this your first motorhome?"

"No, the first one we owned was almost exactly like yours. Truck too. Went out on our first cross-country trip and discovered it wasn't for us."

"Why's that?"

"They're too big and don't go where you want to go. Also, I kept backing into things."

"I hear ya."

"Soups on."

Rose's voice next to Larry brought him back to the hotdogs cooking on the grill. "We'll talk later."

"I'll have Shirley talk to you too. She loves driving the new rig."

Larry piled the meat on the platter, all the while contemplating what John said. *Yes, I'll talk to your wife, if it gets Rosie to drive. I'm in.*

"If my hubby ever takes his hands off of the brats and hotdoggies and sits down, we'll pray."

"Sorry."

Ben prayed over the food and the rest of the evening they talked about their different adventures. Larry promised himself, when their new friends went home, that he'd thank Ben, Betsy and Rose for not discussing the two miscues he'd had with his 5th wheel.

No need to. John and Dwayne shared plenty of their own misfortunes. One in particular almost made Larry cry.

"I'm in Oregon, getting ready to go to the Crescent Cove KOA. MapQuest tells me to turn left. I did. Two hours later, and finding out I can back up a thirty-eight foot 5th wheel on a narrow, gravel road, we're parked in our shady spot at the park."

"You poor thing," Rose said as she walked over to the cooler. "Anyone else want more water?"

"No, we better call it a night. Sounds like you four have a busy day tomorrow." Dwayne stood up and grabbed his chair.

Nicole took a hold of her chair and said, "We got lots to do too, since we're taking off day after tomorrow to Pensacola."

"Day after tomorrow?" Shirley asked. Surprise etched all over her face.

"That's the plan we talked about yesterday."

"Must have been sleeping."

"Good night and thanks for the invite. Betsy, I love your potato salad. I need to get her recipe."

"I'll write it down for you. Talk to you later."

Rose rushed over and gave them all a hug and said, "Just in

case time gets away from us and we don't see each other again."

Larry heard their laughter as they left the campsite. The Early Birds cleared off the table and set the cooler inside Ben's basement compartment. Along with their canvas chairs.

"Can't believe it. Larry, you talked so much, I didn't get my S'mores."

"Since I'm not blabbing anymore, do you want me to get the chairs out again?" Larry reached for the compartment door.

"No need. Rose said for us to come in for some brownies."

"Hey, I'm not giving up my dessert. There's only a few left." Larry rushed over and blocked his front door.

"If I gave up most of Betsy's potato salad to you and people I didn't know; this is the least you can do." Ben walked toward Larry's RV.

He opened the door for him, still not believing his wife would give the last of his treats away. Since she'd had the audacity to do such a thing, there'd better be ice cream on top of his brownie when he sat down to enjoy it.

They walked in and smack dab in the center of his bowl sat a pint of frozen yogurt and he said what any man would say, "I'm not eating that—"

"That scrumptious delight has your name written all over it."

"Does not. The only thing written on this package is it's putrid. And, the yogurt could ruin everything else in our refrigerator it sits next to." He opened the door to peek inside. "See, I told you. The cottage cheese has fur growing on it."

"The reason it grows hairs, old man - we buy it and no one eats the healthy stuff. Case in point. Eating the evils of this world makes it impossible to fit into..."

Larry saw a tear roll down Rose's cheek. "Hon, what are we talking about?"

"A leather coat snuck up behind her and ever since she's been kind of cranky. Ben, it's time to go home. Rose can fill Larry in on what I'm talking about after we leave."

"Can I take my brownie?"

"Be sure to take the yogurt with you too."

"Leave it set, Benjamin. Larry and I are going to eat it even if it kills us."

Larry weighed his response, but went for it anyway since he

had witnesses. "Dear, I'm not sure this product will knock us off. But you serving it to me instead of ice cream, I'm not sure how many more days you'll have left on this earth."

Rose walked to the freezer and took out a half-gallon container of Blue Bell Vanilla Bean ice cream. Larry watched her dip out an ample serving on all four brownies sitting in the dishes in front of her.

No one said a word as she reached for her dish and sauntered to the table and sat down. Before she took her first bite she said, "Am I going to have to eat this all by myself? If so, I hope you can live with the consequences of my kicking the bucket from my cholesterol numbers going through the roof."

The laughter died off the second they all sat down at the table and attacked the much-improved goodie. Larry thought the clinking of spoons in the bowl almost had a rhythm to it. A sweet, straight to your arteries, kind of music.

*Maybe Willie can write another song to this tune.*

Larry reached over and took a bite out of Rose's ice cream and she swatted his arm. He covered her hand with his and said, "Hon, I promise I'll make better choices."

"I can only hope. Remember our discussion the other day, concerning your BP. I don't want to find out how to get along without you. Those two over there." Rose pointed at Ben and Betsy. "Don't look like they'd be much help in eating healthy either."

Rose finished her speech and whipped another spoon out of her pocket. With one in each hand, she reached over and took a spoonful from the bowls sitting across from her.

"Rose, I cannot laugh and enjoy my indulgence. You need to quit."

"Sorry, Bets. Won't say another word until we're done."

The four ate in silence and when the bowls sat empty, Betsy announced, "We need to get home. Matilda is ready for her t.r.e.a.t. too. Aren't you, sweetie?"

Larry almost forgot Ben brought his pooch inside after she'd sat with them outside all evening. Stranger still, Rose left Baby out and she'd behaved around their new friends. A miracle and one he hoped would continue.

Bets put their dishes in the sink and said on her way to the door. "I'll see you in the morning, Rosie. Now, I need to call Mom. Got lots to tell her."

"Concerts, meeting a star. You've got tons to write about too. Get busy."

"You're such a taskmaster."

"Betsy, I've been meaning to ask you about the blog. Is Willie in it?" Ben scooted his wife to the open door.

"I'll tell you about it when we get home. Thanks, guys."

"Any time."

Larry laughed at his wife and Betsy's bantering. They truly fit the word Rose always called them. Pips. He'd found the word in the dictionary. The definition read, 'Ding, dingdong, ding-dong, squawk.'

"Yep, fits them like a glove."

"If you're interested, it was a leather coat. Which I might add – fit anything, but me."

Not sure what that had to do with the subject they'd been talking about, and then he remembered the tear on his wife's cheek.

"Here, hon, let me clean up the dishes and I'll be right over."

*Since I got an extra scoop of ice cream on my brownie, I'm all ears.*

CHAPTER NINE

"Did you call your mom last night?"

"I did. She asked me if we wanted her to come to Mississippi to help us out."

Since Rose couldn't drive and talk at the same time and they'd left early, she pulled her truck into the parking lot next to the beach and asked, "What did you tell your mother?"

"Told her to stay put. That we're still coming. Only delayed a few days."

"I think I can. I think I can."

"What in the world does *Thomas the Train* have to do with us going to Florida."

Rosie stayed quiet, waiting and watching her friend. The moment came. Betsy's eyes grew wide. "I get it. The way it looks right now, we're not going to make it. But we're giving it our best shot."

"Girl, you're starting to think more like me every day."

"Not sure that's something to celebrate."

"Oh ha. Ha."

"Just saying."

Rose put her truck in reverse and in less than five minutes they pulled into the church parking lot. Still a bit early, she enjoyed the scene in front of them. The tide rolled in and out and the early morning visitors scampered away to avoid getting their feet wet.

So many summers as a kid she'd go with her parents to the lakes in Kansas. One of her dad's friends owned a boat. Fun, unless you stayed out too long. Mom always packed the aloe, ready to put on her sunburn. She'd give her a gentle hug after she'd smooth it in.

"Tap, tap, tap."

Rose glanced out her window and Betsy stood there with her fingers in her ears, wiggling them and sticking out her tongue. After rolling down the window she asked her friend, "What are you doing?"

"I could ask the same."

"I'm reminiscing. I hear it's good medicine for what ails you."

"Tell me all about it." Bets leaned in and put her elbows on the door.

"Having to handle clothing I can't even pray to get in, but after my talk with Larry, and the Lord, last night, I'm okeedokie once again."

"I thought I was the one who helped you over the hump."

Rose laughed when Betsy put her lower lip out in a pout. She then said to her friend, "Bets, you helped, however after I ate half of the Blue Bell inventory we had in our freezer, I needed a little bit more convincing that Jesus loves me. Someone with skin on helped."

"I know the feeling. Hubbies are great that way."

"How about we go in and see who we can bless today."

Rose walked beside Bets to the basement of the church, turning on the lights as they made their way to the empty common area.

"Guess we're a little early."

"Gives you time to show me the ropes."

After going over some of the paperwork for about fifteen minutes, Rose decided to broach the subject of Betsy's writing. Find out if the writer's block she'd been suffering from still came a calling.

*Be subtle, Rosie.*

"Making any progress on you know what?" Rose stepped away from the table she'd been working on.

"You know what, what?"

"Mrs. Stevenson, you know what's what?"

"Rosie, I have no idea why I'm not writing my blog. Or anything else, for that matter."

"Even with Willie's concert and singing the song with him? Those two things should give your creativity a much needed oomph. So much so, we'd have trouble keeping up with you."

Rose could almost see the spark starting to light in her friend's eyes. She took another step and said, "How about when you drove the Albatross? There's a Bible lesson shouting about maneuvering fifty-five feet of OH MY GOODNESS."

Rosie's last statement must have tickled Betsy, or it caused her to forget how to speak. A few minutes went by before Bets said, "Yep, I need to write a blog about how I lied to my friend, saying I'd never drive the beast. That'd make a very spiritual post. Don't you think?"

"When you put it that way, you'd better find another topic." Rose took Betsy's hand. "Hon, we need to keep praying. Get this pesky writer's block done and over with. There's a book inside of you waiting to get out."

"But I'm not sure I ca—"

"Can, what? Write a novel?" The verse from the historical novel she'd been reading came to mind and she recited it to her friend. *"You can do ALL things through…"* She motioned for Bets to finish it.

*"through Christ who strengthens me."*

"See that wasn't so hard."

"Rosie, I don't know what I'd do without your words of wisdom."

"If you haven't noticed, there are people all around me who need my expert help in their time of distress. Looks like I've done it again."

"Hello, ladies." Linda stood at the door. Her arms laden with clothes in every color of the rainbow.

"What did you bring us?" Rose hurried over to help her.

Linda handed a few items to Rose and said, "I wanted to bring a few items for Katy and go over a few things before we take Everly to the shop."

"I can't wait to see what today brings." Rose did a jig on the tan-colored Berber carpet under her feet then she stopped and checked to see if anyone caught her. "Are they okay with dancing in this church?"

"You're fine and I believe you're ready to go." Linda smiled. "But, before we go, I want to tell you what the Lord has put on my heart. After talking to my husband, I realized I'm approaching this ministry all wrong. I'm looking at the working woman. Not her as a whole."

Rose picked up a pair of peach capris and a shirt with sage and coral in it. "Is this what you're talking about?"

"Exactly. I don't know about you two ladies, but giving them casual wear, as well as the business attire, will take their lives up a notch. Change their mindset in everything they do from this point forward."

"I'm in. What a great idea."

"Betsy, when Kate comes by today to get the leather coat, show her the clothes I brought today. She can take whatever works for her."

"Sounds like a plan. Now you and Rosie better get out of here. There's a bunch of women ready to get their lives back on track."

"Bets, you're absolutely right. We do need to get going. Linda, I'll follow you in my truck. No need for you to bring me back here."

"And miss out on seeing how the women look when they put all the outfits together. Not a chance."

Before they headed out, Rose took the clothes the store owner brought Kate and put them in one of the classrooms. Without turning on the light, she placed them on the table in the center of the room. She knew Betsy would straighten them out after Linda and she left.

Rosie couldn't get over the fact that the Lord had put them there. No mirror hung on the church wall, but if there'd been one, and she could see herself – she'd be grinning from ear to ear.

Actually her cheeks ached from doing it so much. Rose turned to leave and ran smack dab into Betsy.

"What are you all smiles about?"

"Praising the Lord in all circumstances, that's all."

"In dark rooms. Are you sure the clothes aren't in a heap in the middle of the floor?"

"I'm sure…ye of little faith. Talk to you later."

***

Linda turned on the lights when they reached Sassy Seconds. Straight in front of Rose on the wall hung the plaques. Before she forgot she asked, "Linda, who is responsible for these works of art. Did you make them?"

"Me, some artist friends, and my heavenly Father."

"Great team."

"I think so, too."

Rose peered at the expansive wall display and she could almost feel the presence of the Lord and said so. Again, the shop owner's smile lit up the room and she said, "Thank you."

"No thank you." Rose went over and plucked one off the wall. "This one's for Betsy. An early Christmas present." Taking the *Jesus Loves Me* one down she announced, "And, this one's all mine."

"Take them. You two have blessed me more than you'll ever know."

"Won't hear of it." Rose reached in her fanny pack and brought out a credit card. "Here you go."

Rose watched as the woman wrapped up her purchases and again admired the talent it took to master the quality and beauty of each different sign.

"I'll put your bag back here and when we get ready to head to the church later, I'll remind you to get it."

Rose nodded, but her mind idled on something else and she smiled at her new friend before she said, "Linda, we need to take these national. People have to see these beauties."

"No, they're doing fine right here."

"Is that right? How many have you sold?"

Linda glanced in the direction of the signs as if they'd answer the question Rosie asked. Then she tapped on the counter, next to the register, with her index finger.

"Dear, I'm not asking you to give me your yearly sales. I'm wondering how many you've sold."

"As of two minutes ago. About twenty-five. Maybe a few more. Why? Do you know someone?"

Rose froze in her tracks when she saw Linda's expression. Betsy had worn the same one the night they saw Willie Nelson. But, at the moment, though, the store owner's guise won First

Prize—with votes left to tally.

*Help me, Lord. I'm about to burst her bubble.*

"Rose, is there something wrong?"

"Linda, I'm fine. However, about your plaques. I don't know anyone who can take your precious signs to the masses. Guess we can say once again – I was flapping my chops for no reason other than to hear myself talk."

"Please don't worry about it, Rose. I'm happy to sell the signs here in my shop."

Rose felt horrible. Once again she'd spoken before her thought process caught up with her mouth. Or whatever you wanted to call it. She couldn't wait to tell Betsy. Hopefully she'd have some helpful advice for her at the end of the day. Again.

Preferably how to keep her trap shut.

Rosie imagined their conversation when Bets asked what she did all day. *Oh, I dashed someone's dream when I asked them a simple question. You should have seen it. I broke her heart like it was a weathered twig scattered on the ground after a wind storm.*

"It's really okay, Rose. We do need to get to work." Linda gave her a smile and a hug. "I make the signs for people like you and Bets. It blesses me that you love them so much."

"No doubt about it."

Rosie followed Linda to the back of the expansive shop. Stacks of specific-colored clothing, lay on dozens of tables in and around the large warehouse attached to the second-hand store.

The blue, red and green tables stood in a U-shape to Rose's left. When she turned to her right, she spied three more tables with blacks, browns and beige clothes on them. Almost overwhelmed at the sight, Rosie took a deep breath to make sure she didn't faint dead away.

"Why didn't Betsy tell me about this?"

"She wanted to surprise you."

"That's an understatement." Rose found a chair and took a seat.

"Douglas, give this woman some water. We're about to lose her," Linda yelled at her assistant who'd walked in at that precise moment.

"On it."

Rose watched the man drop the hanger he carried in and

become a sprinter in five easy steps. He ran around the tables placed in the room and in record time returned with a bottle of water and gave it to Rosie. And a smile to boot.

"That was quite a show."

"Do it all the time. People are always coming in here. I say they're awe struck. You're the first one to turn completely pale. I'll open the back door and get some coastal breezes going through here."

After a few sips of water, Rose felt among the living again. The chocolate chip cookie Linda brought her, straight from the oven, also helped to cure all that ailed her. And left her to wonder if there were some Keebler elves living in the back of the store.

Rose chuckled, but kept the elfin observation to herself and said, "Thank you" to the store owner and enjoyed the mouth-watering delight. Even going as far as to lick her fingers for the last bit of crumbs when she finished it.

"I love the sweet smell of cookie's baking. Reminds me of my grandmother." Rose stood, keeping one hand on the table.

"Please rest for now. Everly called while I was in the kitchen and said she'd be here in about a half hour. Her measurements are on the sheet and it won't take long to pick out what will work out for her when she gets here."

Rose didn't need to sit anymore. While she waited for the woman, she decided to take advantage of the extra time. She gazed at a whole lot of clothing items and selected a few after she got the younger woman's measurements off of her paperwork.

After collecting some cuter-than-cute outfits for her charge, Rose perused the black table a little bit more. One item tickled her fingertips when she touched it.

The velvet evening jacket with blue-topaz buttons and a cream-colored shell lined with silk on the next table stopped Rose in her tracks. She stepped to get a closer look and said, "Linda, I'm going to have to quit working here or lose fifty pounds. These two items, they're perfect for an evening out with your special someone."

"That's why I do this."

"And it shows in everything you do."

Rose didn't want to back the wagon up to what they'd talked about earlier, but her own heart still ached for her new friend.

More people needed to see her works of art and know the plaques existed.

*But how, Lord? I need Your help on this one.*

"Hi, Linda."

"Everly, I'm so glad to see you. Come over and meet Miss Rose."

Rose saw a beautiful woman walking toward her who stood no more than five-foot three inches, if she wore high heels. Her weight evenly distributed in a pear-shaped package of red curls and freckles. No doubt, they'd get along fine and dandy.

All morning and into the early afternoon Rose, and Linda on occasion, dressed and redressed Everly. Finding the right hues for her crimson locks took some time, but in the end they mastered the task.

Rose tucked in a tag and said, "Young lady, if I had the need for an assistant on the road, I'd hire you in a minute. You're going to knock the corporate world on its ear. With what I read about your grades in college, they'll be impressed too."

"When you grow up with a houseful of siblings, you escape when you can. Mine was the bedroom I shared with my baby sister. I'd spend hours in there studying and dreaming of my future. Summers, my parents sent me to my aunt's house in Naples. She still lives there."

"Don't mean to interrupt, sweetie, but that's close to where we're going after we leave here. Please give me her name and I'll call her when we get down there."

"Rose, she'd love you to come over for a visit. Wish my aunt still had her store. Such a fun place to see. Antiques and discarded items covered half a city block." Everly laughed.

"A junk yard?"

"Not exactly. More organized piles. I helped her in the summer for two weeks. Taught me everything I know. I hope my daughter and I can go visit one day."

"I'm sure she'd love that."

"What my aunt wants is for us to move down there, but right now I'm working on what's next here in Biloxi. To better myself and for..." Everly paused and took out her phone and showed Rose her fifteen-year old daughter. "Her name is Olivia."

"Oh, what a pretty, pretty girl."

"Miss Rose, you're so kind. People do tell me I should take her to Hollywood. She'd be a star, but I'll pass. The Lord has us here in Mississippi and we're happy right where He's put us."

"We're glad too," Linda said as she appeared at the back door. "Now, ladies, it's time to go to church."

"On Thursday afternoon?"

Everly laughed and Linda gave Rose a sideward glance. "Don't forget your early Christmas presents."

Rose got her sack from behind the counter and followed the two women out of the store. Linda had almost reached her car when Rosie called to her, "Can we go back inside. I forgot something."

"Sure. Everly go ahead and get in. We'll be right back...I think."

"Won't take long."

And it didn't. Rose already had the plaque picked out for Everly. Linda took it off the wall and wrapped it.

"Yes, Joshua 24:15 is perfect. "But as for me and my household, we will serve the Lord."

"She'll love it."

"I'm counting on it."

*And I'm counting on you Lord to help us find places to sell these treasures.*

CHAPTER TEN

Larry, a dollop of mud is running down your neck."

"Thought some of it dropped on me. Can you wipe it off? Kind of hard for me to get it."

Larry stood still while Ben used his trowel to take off the drywall texture and put it back in the trough they shared.

"There you go. All clean and fresh."

"This is the last coat in this room, which means we are almost done with the addition. A few days over schedule, but as you know - perfection takes time." Larry laughed.

"You missed a spot."

Ben and Larry spun around and Jeff and Mary stood in front of them, next to the door. They rushed over and hugged them. Neither worrying if they'd got drywall mud on the returning Early Birds.

"I thought Rosie said you'd meet us in Florida? Do our wives know you're here?"

"No, we wanted to surprise you. Rosie texted Mary the other day and said you'd be working here at the church," Jeff said as he grabbed Larry's trowel and went to work on smoothing out a spot on the wall.

"Thanks."

"You guys do good work."

"And lots of it," the pastor said as he came into the new sanctuary.

"Hey, Steve, let me introduce you to our friends. Jeff and Mary."

"Nice to meet you. Listening to Ben and Larry, the RV lifestyle is sounding better every day. Since we lost everything in the fire—it's an option."

"We lost our home in a flood in Colorado."

"Larry told me the other day. Guess you can say I understand your situation. Gotta run. Great meeting both of you."

Steve walked out and for the next ten minutes Jeff and Mary told them about their travels to Mississippi.

"You know you're going to repeat all of this to the girls when you see them tonight. That's after they recover from the shock of seeing you here."

"I can't wait to see Bets and Rose. I've missed them," Mary said.

"We'll all be home in about three hours."

"How about we let you get back to work. We'll see you at the RV Park around 4:30 or 5:00. Supper's on us tonight."

"Music to our ears."

"While we're out, do you need any supplies? Some fixings for S'mores, Ben?"

"You had to ask him. Now I won't get any work out of him the rest of the day."

"I'll be fine, Mr. Wilford. I'm not the one who had to have their work tweaked a few minutes ago."

"Great seeing you and we better scoot before we start talking again."

Jeff and Mary headed out the door and Ben and Larry went back to work. Neither saying anything for about two minutes then his friend said, "The Early Birds are back together again."

"And the sooner we finish here, Ben, the sooner we can sit and chat with both of them again."

They worked with a renewed fervor for the next two hours, so when the pastor came in and told them to get out of there, Larry almost jumped into the bucket of mud standing next to them.

"Guess it's time to clean up."

Ben emptied the trough into the five-gallon bucket and took

Larry's trowel to the kitchen sink to clean it.

Larry gathered their trash and ten minutes later they made their way through traffic to the Tadpole RV Park. When he drove in he said, "Not sure where they parked them, but hope it's near us."

"Don't believe so. There's another Class C parked next to you. Not a trailer like they had."

"I'll call Jeff and he'll tell us where to find them."

"Or we won't have supper."

"Or S'mores."

"If you don't quit reminding me, I'm going to fix them for dinner. And not share."

Larry parked his truck and pulled out his cell phone. Before he dialed his friend's number, Jeff stood next to his truck. His large frame almost blocked his exit out the door, but he managed to get out of his vehicle and take a gander at the other RVs.

"What are you looking for?"

"Your trailer?"

"It's right here."

"That's not a trailer." Ben moved closer to the motorhome.

"That's the business we had to finish in Colorado. Sold the other one to a man in Lyons and we bought this one."

"Good thing you didn't buy the 25 footer. Like over there." Larry pointed at their neighbor's rig. "Your legs would stick out a good foot off the bed in that one."

"Mary had me lay on the bed in the smaller unit and my feet did hang over a good bit." Jeff laughed.

"The extra few feet to have the bedroom is worth it for my hubby."

"We still got you beat." Ben touched the side of his RV. "Plenty of room to stretch out in this monster."

"Yea, fifty-five feet of too much trouble. For some of us – me. I'm beginning to think smaller is the ticket."

*What's the point of such a big rig anyway?*

Larry heard a squeal and decided it came from one person or persons. Betsy and Rose had made it home.

"Who do we have here?" Rose scurried over and gave them a hug.

Betsy took her turn and said, "So good to see you two."

"They're making us dinner tonight."

"Ben, is food the only thing on your mind these days?"

"No, but since I'm not working as much, I've got to do something. Food seems the subject I like to ponder on the most."

"Hon, you're working on something, but we'll talk about that later." Betsy walked over and patted her hubby's midsection and laughed.

"Will you two behave? We haven't seen these two in a month and we start off the conversation talking about Ben's waistline. We'll pick that one up for another day."

"Rosie, you have no idea how much we've missed you."

"I'll second that."

"Make it a third."

Betsy hugged both of the newcomers again and said, "Me four."

"So glad you haven't changed." Jeff sat in a lawn chair and extended his legs out in front of him.

"Us? If anything, we've gotten worse." Rose laughed.

"Some of us more than others and I'm not naming names."

Larry glanced at his wife and wanted to say something, but the sun setting over the Gulf of Mexico changed his retort. Instead he shouted, "Spectacular sunset. All eyes due west, or you'll miss it."

He went in search of his 35mm camera and found it about ten minutes later in the bottom of their pantry. Within seconds, Larry dashed back down the stairs and across the major road, making sure no traffic ran into him on the way across.

As he positioned his camera to take the shot, he stopped. In his view finder stood Mary, Rose and Betsy taking a selfie. As always, dramatics played a bigger part in the proceedings than the actual photo taking.

Larry tapped his foot on the sand and waited, and then he said, "Can you three move? I'd like to get a shot today."

Rose kicked some sand in his direction, but kept standing in the exact spot with her friends. They turned to take another shot of themselves before moving a few feet to their left. Giggles followed them down the beach.

"Thank you."

Larry said the words to the ladies, but mostly to his heavenly Father for giving them such a stupendous sunset. Yellow, reds, oranges exploded in the western sky. If he dared to blink, the scene in front of him would change, giving him another photo opportunity.

The cool breeze off the ocean and the surf lapping at the sand almost made him forego dinner and bring his chaise lounge over. To relax. Take an evening snooze, but his stomach said otherwise. It rumbled and Larry realized he hadn't eaten lunch. Too busy mudding.

When the last glimpse of the sun disappeared into the ocean, they all crossed Highway 90 to their campsites. Larry didn't know about the others, but he could have eaten a side of beef all by himself.

About the time he went to open his mouth to say what crossed his mind, one of their neighbors yelled over, "Hey, why don't all of you join us for our last-night-here celebration? We have plenty of fixins'."

After moving chairs around and filling their plates, most of the Early Birds settled in around the fire. The sweet smell of barbeque filled the air and Larry's mouth watered as he put a dollop of beans next to his beef sandwich and corn on the cob. He was ready to chow down.

"Larry, since you're the last to sit down, why don't you pray?"

He prayed and when he finished, he settled into his seat. Ready to dig into his plate of food. But the sound of the Gulf of Mexico captured his attention again. Larry couldn't wait to review the pictures he'd taken earlier.

"Your food's getting cold."

"Rosie, you know I've always been a fan of cold roast beef sandwiches."

"In another life." She reached over and touched his arm. "Thanks for the prayer. The Lord's traveling angels will definitely watch over these four when they take off tomorrow morning."

"I sure hope so. We can always use some help out on the road." Larry smiled then added, "The Lord also makes some pretty amazing sunsets. Tonight was one of His best."

"You're right about that too."

Larry dug into his meal and every so often he had to wipe the barbeque sauce off his chin to keep it from dribbling down on his work shirt. The one he'd have to wear again tomorrow. The laundry fairy hadn't appeared in their campground. Yet.

"Here, hon, tuck this in your collar." Rose handed him a heavy-duty napkin and leaned in closer to him and said in a quieter tone, "FYI—the laundry fairy, she's on her way and should complete her job, oh in a day or two."

"Looking forward to her arrival. Or, if you're so inclined, bring me something home from Sassy Seconds to wear."

"I'll take a look tomorrow. There's sure to be something in your size."

Larry chuckled when he heard the familiar sound his wife made when she got tickled. He assumed her reaction had a little to do with their discussion of needing to do laundry. But more of what she'd pick out for him at the second-hand store.

He envisioned glitter, or some such thing that included something shiny. Not a chance and with that Larry opened the oversized napkin Rosie gave him and stuck the one end of it in his shirt collar and finished his meal.

"Can I interest anyone in S'mores?"

He decided to ignore Ben's announcement and let his food settle for a minute or two. While Larry waited, he decided to try to catch John and get more information about his smaller Class C.

The opportunity came when he saw his new friend head over to the fire. Larry followed him and said, "When we're done here, can I ask you some more questions about your rig?"

"Sure can."

They joined everyone as they huddled around the fire pit to fix their gooey dessert. Larry promised himself he'd have one…maybe two, but lost count after four. But his now-tighter-than-normal belt around his middle reminded him he'd over indulged.

The urge to change into his sweatpants almost overtook him, but he refrained. At the moment he had more important things to do. First: Try not to alert Rosie of what he was about to do. Second: Larry had to get John away from the others without much fanfare.

He accomplished it…barely. The over-her-glasses stare from Rose when he asked, "John, since you fix wrecked cars, can you take a look at the back of my trailer?" This almost brought the proceedings to a standstill.

Thankfully John went along and followed Larry behind his 5th wheel. Once they got away from his nosy wife he said, "I don't want Rosie to know I'm even considering trading this in. What do you like and don't like about this one? The size? Whatever it is, tell me."

For the next ten minutes John filled Larry's mind with chassis information, pros and cons of having a truck and trailer versus one unit to drive around. "If you want, you can tow a vehicle behind it."

John even touched on the size of the bed in the twenty-five footer and said, "If you're not ones who cozy up to each other. One of you can sleep on the couch, on the table, or above the cab of the truck."

"No worries there. My Rosie's a cuddlier."

"And why does Mr. Larson need to know this information?"

Larry and John almost knocked each other down trying to make it seem like nothing out of the ordinary had happened. And nothing came to mind that his wife wouldn't ask more questions about.

*Lord, I could use some help here.*

"I'm waiting." Rose crossed her arms at her chest.

*I'm waiting too, but nothing's coming.*

"Rose we got off the subject a bit," John walked to the picnic table and sat down. "Yea, I told him about our bed and he said yours is a—"

"Memory foam," Larry finished his friend's sentence.

"That led to you telling John that I like to cuddle?"

*Rosie, you're killing me.*

Again John came to his rescue. "I said my wife likes to snuggle."

"Oh, that's sweet, but for some reason, gentlemen, I'm not believing a word coming out of your mouths."

Larry watched his wife walk away before turning to John. Both had to suppress their laughter until Rosie got far enough away.

"See what I mean. She's like a tiger. Sneaks around behind her prey and will devour them before they know what hit them."

"I'll wait until we're on the road tomorrow, but I have to share this with Shirley."

"Be sure to tell her not to text Rosie about it until I've let you know we've bought our own."

"Deal."

He and John parted ways and Larry went to find Rose. His goal was to smooth over any more concerns she might voice about his meeting with John. But when he found his wife, she ignored him. No questions at all.

*No cuddling for me tonight.*

## CHAPTER ELEVEN

"Not sure what Larry's doing, but my radar's on full-alert mode."

Rose jabbered with Betsy and Mary as she drove down Highway 90 to Sassy Seconds Friday morning. They needed to stop there to check with Linda. To see what she had planned for them that day.

Mary leaned in between the seats at one point and asked Rosie, "Why do you think Larry's doing anything out of the ordinary?"

"Mr. Introvert does not discuss our sleeping habits or positions with anyone. Especially someone he met three days ago."

"Does seem strange, Rosie. As long as I've known your hubby, even joking with him about you know what..." Betsy stopped and shook her head from side to side. "Not that it's a subject we talk about often, or ever. Oh, forget it. I'm getting myself in deeper the more I talk."

"Yes, and enough with talking trash. You two need to shush so I can tell you about the dream I've had the last two nights. About Linda's plaques. We've got to put our heads together and figure out how more people can see them. It's like the Lord's gnawing on me and won't let me sleep until I do something."

"Thought you were looking a little ragged."

Betsy turned to the backseat so fast it almost gave Rosie

whiplash. But since she drove the vehicle, she'd wait to gawk at their rear-seat passenger after coming to a stop at Linda's shop.

But on the way there, though, the cab of the truck held enough laughter to fill Royal Stadium. Rosie lost count after ten snorts. When she pulled into the parking lot, she mentioned the fact, making them laugh even louder inside the dually.

"Stop it. I can't see to park."

"Use the large building in front of you to put it in a parking spot. It's early. No one else is here, except us professional dressers."

"And one tagging along."

"Who we're glad is here. We've missed you."

"Us too, but back to your idea of getting the plaques out. I've got the perfect person. My niece, Jennifer. She has a store in Estes Park."

"Lord, You are amazing. So are you, Mary."

"Don't get too excited. I still need to call Jenny and send her some pictures."

Rose opened her door, but before she stepped out she ventured a peek in the back seat. "Mary, once you see them, you'll want to buy one or more to take to your niece."

"Unless you buy them all before her." Betsy laughed when she opened her door and got out. Mary followed.

Rose met the ladies at the front of the truck. "I did purchase one, or more," Rose covered her mouth to hide the last part. "I plan to give Everly hers today."

"Did I hear my name."

"You did and it's all good. Everly, I'd like you to meet Mary. Our friend from Colorado I told you about."

"I'm sorry to hear about you losing your house in the flood."

"Thanks, but it's funny. Some days I forget it happened. The Lord is so faithful."

"He is that, for sure."

"Since Jeff and Mary only got in late yesterday, we haven't had a chance to tell her much about what we're doing with you and the other precious ladies."

"Whatever it is you're doing, Rose, I want in."

"Well, then, let's go in and meet everyone else." Rose took Mary's hand and led her toward Sassy Seconds. Betsy tagged along behind.

Douglas opened the front door for them and said, "Linda's in the back and has more things for you."

"She does?"

"I do too, but we'll talk later." Rose couldn't wait to see her face when she saw the plaque. She hoped that it went with the décor in the tiny apartment she said she rented.

"I'm amazed at how the Lord continues to bless me."

"Amen."

Rose laughed when everyone, including Douglas, shouted out the one-word proclamation. But what made her smile even more was when the young man came from behind the counter and took Everly's hand in his.

From the smile on her face, the younger woman must not have seen anything wrong with his forthrightness. At one point, Rose decided a person couldn't slide a piece of paper between the two of them.

They stood cozy in the far corner until Linda came out from the backroom and announced to everyone in attendance, "Is there a party going on out here? Why wasn't I invited?"

The store owner smiled, but Douglas must not have seen Linda's merriment. In a split second he moved behind the counter. Rose assumed he relocated before his boss told him the time of day.

*I hope Douglas knows Everly's got a teenager at home?*

Someone's phone rang, interrupting Rose's thoughts. She reached for hers, but found the screen black. The incessant sound quit when Betsy swiped her screen and said, "It's my mom. I'll take it outside."

Rose introduced Mary to Linda and the three of them went out to the warehouse. Everly tried on more outfits, coming out to model each one.

"Linda, the capris are the perfect fit. Did you get a donation from teen girls this time?" Everly laughed at her own joke.

"No, I bought these for you. I ran to the store after work and these two pieces jumped in my cart. Didn't see a reason to stop them."

Everly ran over and hugged her. "I love them."

"They'll work for the office or…when you go out on a date

with…whoever that might be."

Rose decided if a face had the ability to flush ten different colors in a split second, Everly took the prize for getting it done. Along with her curly red hair, she blazed like a bonfire at a college fraternity party.

"He's cute, but…"

"Trust in the Lord, Everly. He'll direct your paths." Rose snapped her fingers. "Yes, that's the sign she needs. I want to exchange the one I bought yesterday. No, I want that one too."

"She goes on like that all the time," Betsy said when she came back in the room. "You'll get used to her the more you get to know her."

"Thought there was something wrong with Miss Rose?"

"Heavens no, Everly, I am peachy. However, ignore Betsy. She's mad 'cause she missed out on some goings on while she gabbed on her phone. Now if we're done in here, there's something else I need to buy."

Rose led the way back into the front of the store and pointed at the plaques on the wall. "There they are, Mary. Aren't they spectacular?"

"You described them, Rosie, but seeing them. WOW. Is it okay if I take some pictures? I want to text my niece. She'll love these. I know it."

"Told ya so. And, Douglas, while she's taking pictures, please get me down the plaque with I Thessalonians 29:11 on it."

He rang up Rose's purchase then climbed the two-tiered footstool to bring down the gift she requested. All the while he smiled at Everly. When he landed back on the floor, Douglas turned the sign and read it out loud.

*"For I know the plans I have for you,"* declares the Lord, *"plans to prosper you and not to harm you, plans to give you hope and a future."*

"Thank you, son." Rose took a tissue out of her purse and dabbed at her eyes. "We've had ourselves a church service here at Sassy Seconds today. And speaking of church, we need to go. First Baptist Church is waiting for us."

"I also want to see what our guys are doing. That's after I take another picture, or two here." Mary moved over to the wall display again and put her phone up and started clicking away.

"When Phyllis Photog is done, we'll hit the road."

"I'm almost finished."

Rose grabbed Everly's hand this time and they went out to her truck. "Come here, dear."

She gave her the bag with the plaque and Everly unwrapped the tissue. Rose heard a gasp and the young woman said, "Joshua 25:15 is my favorite verse. Rosie, they're perfect. Both of them. Thank you."

Everly hugged Rose with such enthusiasm that her glasses flew clean off her nose and hit the asphalt and bounced. "Oh, I'm so sorry, Rosie. Let me get them for you." She reached down and picked them up off the pavement.

"Hon, I did almost the same thing at Willie Nelson's concert. Difference there, the man's glasses only dangled off one of his ears when I got done with him. They didn't fly across the parking lot like mine did. This is not a problem, dear, they are readers". Rose smiled and gave Everly another hug.

Betsy stepped in and said, "Church. You said we need to—"

"Get going." Rose stepped away. "Yes, we do, but Everly it was such a pleasure meeting you. Take care of Olivia and we'll pray...no, we'll pray for you right now."

Rose took off on a prayer that continued their church service in the parking lot of the second-hand store. When she stopped, all of them wiped their eyes and said, "Amen."

"Thanks again, Rose and it was great meeting all of you."

"Bye, dear. We'll keep in touch."

Rosie unlocked her truck and almost had herself hoisted on the seat when she remembered something. "Girls, I'll be right back."

She hurried to the store again. A mission needed accomplished. Douglas still stood at the front counter and Rose embarked on his agenda first.

"Son, I don't pull any punches. If your heart is where it needs to be with the Lord then I say, 'Bless your pea-picking heart as any good Texan says'."

"Huh?"

"You dating Everly, silly."

Rose watched his face go from tan to a pasty color and in the end turned red to the top of his own curly do.

"Thank you, ma'am. I hope to take care of Everly and Olivia for the rest of my life, if she'll have me."

"You follow the Lord and He'll lead you. Like the verse I gave her. Heed those words. A side-note, son, if you haven't noticed - she's interested."

Douglas performed a move she'd never seen before, but if she had to name it, she'd call it a true, blue quick step performed by a man in L.O.V.E.

"Linda, I need another sign. This one's for your employee. Move away, Douglas, it's not proper for you to ring in your own present."

Rose directed the store owner to the plaque on the bottom row. The words of First Corinthians 13:4-8, clearly the best advice for the new couple.

*Love is patient. Love is kind. And so much more...*

"Douglas, remember these verses and you'll be where the Lord wants you at all times."

"I promise, ma'am. Thank you."

The man's smile melted Rose's heart and she rushed over and gave him one of her better hugs. Not a run of the mill kind.

"Rosie, here's your receipt and don't forget to hug me before you leave."

"Linda, I couldn't forget you." Rose gave her one for the record books too and said, "See you on Monday. For our final few days."

"If you're not careful I'm going to kidnap you and the rest of the Early Birds. I need you around here. You're good for business."

"Funny you'd bring that up. Mary took some pictures of your plaques." Rose leaned in and whispered, "She knows someone in Estes Park, Colorado. Actually she's related to her. I'm sure her niece will be calling to talk to you. Guess I *do* know someone who knows someone."

"Are you getting the cart before the horse again, Rosie?"

"Not this time. If Mary's niece doesn't come through – I'll jump on a plane to Colorado to straighten out her thinking." Rose smiled. "But I'm not worried. She's going to love them. No doubt about it."

Linda gave her another hug. "If the woman needs to ask me

anything, you've got my number."

"I sure do. See ya soon!"

Rose waltzed out to her truck and told Mary and Bets the details of the last ten minutes. "If I ever thought of adoption, Douglas and Everly, they'd top the charts. I do hope they get together. I'm no marriage professional, but it looks as if they're heading in the right direction."

"Unlike us, at the rate we're going, we won't make it to church for Sunday service two days from now."

Mary's second zinger sent Rose's truck into overdrive and it hadn't moved from the parking spot. With all the giggling going on, the end wouldn't come anytime soon to get them moving.

When Rosie caught her breath she shouted, "If you or Betsy aren't going to stop. I'll have to take the heifers by the horns. Settle yourselves down."

"We're settled."

Rose heard two seat belts fasten and only a few snickers from the passenger's seat and the one behind her.

"Now that's better. There must be one adult in the mix to make this work."

"Rosie is always my choice to help us with adultiness. How about you, Mary?"

"It's a go with this heifer too."

"I give up."

Rose drove along the beach to the First Baptist Church. Every so often she'd hear noise from both seats. She ignored her truck mates and kept her mind on the road and on the colorful kites she saw people flying near the shoreline.

When she pulled in next to Ben's truck, Rose made a note in her phone about flying a kite. Maybe, once they hit Florida, the Early Birds could plan a fun day out on the beach, learning this new task.

"What are you doing, Rosie?"

"Jotting down a fun thing to do here or when we get to Flor-i-da." Rose drug out the last word.

"More fun than spending the day with your best friends?"

"Both are full of wind."

Mary and Betsy gave Rose a strange look, but instead of elaborating on her comment or telling them about kite flying, she left them wondering and said, "There are the guys, sitting at the picnic table."

## CHAPTER TWELVE

"Hi hon. What brings you ladies to church this time of day?"

"Stopping in to see if Jan needed us for anything." Rose sat next to her hubby. "We're running out of ladies to dress. We'll be done the first of next week."

"Rosie, I'm not sure we'll make it until then. We're finishing the painting this afternoon." Ben took a bite of his sandwich.

"We'll put in more hours than the men. I like the sound of that."

"More brownie points for us in heaven, Bets."

Jeff tossed his sack into the trash. "I'm not sure that's biblical."

"It's in the book of Rose, chapter three, verse nine."

"Mary, I'm not sure if it's the water in Mississippi, or what. But you're getting feistier the longer I know you."

"Lack of belongings will do that. I'm free to be me." Mary laughed.

"Along with what my bride said, I've found out the only thing that matters is the ones you love. Not the stuff you have."

"Jeff, I'm touched to know that you love us. Another thing I'm certain of, we're a team of pretty good workers."

"How about the men part of the 'team' getting in there and putting the final coat of paint on the wall. Daylight's a wasting."

100

"We're inside, Lar. Don't need sunshine."

"Ben, you are such a stickler for details." Larry went over and gave his wife a kiss. "We'll see you ladies at home later. Love ya, Rosie."

"Remember, we're feeding everyone tonight, since we didn't get it done last night."

"Whatever the case. We're eating," Ben said as he opened the door to the church.

\*\*\*

The women went in and headed down a long hallway. Larry, Ben and Jeff took the stairs to the second floor. Two five-gallon buckets awaited them in the sanctuary. Larry unwrapped his roller and worked on the last wall. The other two went back to what they'd been doing.

As he painted the final strip and got ready to put his roller to soak, a large spot on the far wall caught his eye. He walked over and raised the roller to remedy the missed area, but realized sun streamed through the steeple-shaped window and draped the wall with a mosaic of color.

It's light illuminated the picture of Jesus, standing at the door knocking. Always one of Larry's favorites. The same painting hung in his hometown church and until his youth leader told him, he hadn't realized the door didn't have a knob on it.

"Are you painting or can we wrap this up and call it a day?"

"I believe we can, Ben."

The three of them went to the basement and cleaned their rollers then put the lids on the paint. Larry reached for one of the five-gallon containers and said, "Steve told me to put the paint in the shed out in the side yard when we finished."

Instead of moving in that direction, Larry watched Ben sit down on his bucket. He presumed his friend sat on it to close it more securely, or needed a rest. Who knew. A few seconds went by and he stood back up and announced to anyone who cared, "Secure."

"Good to know."

They dropped the paint off and Larry surveyed the mess inside the shed. It reminded him of his own garage in Texas. An idea clicked in his mind and he said, "I'm sure the pastor doesn't come out here to do much, but wouldn't it be—"

"We're on it."

"Since I'm too tall to fit in there, I'll carry the trash to the dumpsters." Jeff leaned against the side. "Being tall has its advantages. Other times, it gets in the way."

"Here you go." Ben gave him a bag. "This'll work."

About an hour in, Larry stopped working when he heard a voice coming from outside. He couldn't make out what the person said, so he stuck his head out of the door to listen. That was when he saw Steve hanging halfway out the upstairs window.

"Better not lean out any more or one of us will have to catch you."

"I'm fine, but what are you guys doing?"

"We tried to put the paint away, but there wasn't any place to set it. Me and the boys are making room. Along with doing a few other things."

"Stay there. I'll be right down. I need to talk to you."

"Ah oh! Hope we're not in trouble?" Ben sat on the bucket again. "Larry, if he's mad, offer him one of Rosie's brownies. They always soothe what's troubling me."

"I think everything's okay."

The pastor walked in. "Hey guys, I thought you'd taken off already."

"Nah! My mama taught me not to leave my toys lying around."

"From the job you three did in this shed, she also told you to pick up other people's 'toys' too. I'll thank you, but when Fred sees this place. Watch out."

Larry hoped he meant "watch out" in a good way. Maybe they needed to leave right then before they finished. He smiled at the thought of a maintenance man chasing them with the riding lawn mower, while swinging a hoe out in front of him.

"Not sure what's entertaining you over there, but whatever it is tell us about it."

"Ben, I think Betsy and my wife are rubbing off on me. I just imagined Fred on his John Deere, chasing us down with a piece of lawn equipment in his hand."

"You need to get out more, Lar." Jeff peered into the ten by fifteen shed.

"Don't give me any lip. Just because you can't fit in small

spaces."

"The Lord couldn't contain all the smarts and good looks in an average body. He had to go big."

"The Father filled you with something when He made you, but I believe it has a different name."

"Larry, the word you're searching for is the Holy Spirit."

"Thanks, Steve. That's much better than the word I might have come up with." Larry leaned down and scooped up the empty water bottle he found and tossed it at his tall friend.

Jeff reached down to retrieve the bottle Larry threw at him, but before he got ahold of it Ben grabbed it. "Guys, how about we get back to why Steve came all the way down to see us. What do you say?"

All four laughed and the pastor said, "You guys are finished here. All we need to do is bring in the chairs and tables and the new addition is complete."

"WOOHOO!!!"

"I second what Larry said."

"Thirds from me."

"On Sunday we've planned a Harvest Party, but since we finished ahead of time. It's also a celebration service. I hope all of you can come to it."

"We'll be there," Larry answered for all of them, then visions of his wife flashed in front of his eyes and he asked, "Do the ladies know we're done? If not, they may be hankering to chase all of us with the John Deere in your shed."

"Larry, you're safe. Jan told me she talked to them a little while ago."

"Since we're continuing to jabber out here in the Mississippi heat, how about we go inside where there's some A/C?" Jeff wiped his forehead with the sleeve of his shirt. "I'm not used to this humidity."

"Toughens you up."

"Are you serious, Ben? When we lived in Texas, we had air conditioning in our homes, in our cars, and again at work. It didn't 'toughen' anything in us. More like we became wimpier."

"Whatever the case. Get that door open. I need some water."

"I'll see you guys on Sunday."

A blast of cool air hit Larry, and he watched as his friends ran over to the water fountain. While he stood there, his back and one shoulder shouted that he'd worked them too hard. Thank goodness for some down time to rest and recuperate.

*Then we'll be on the road again.*

"Are you two ready to go home?" Ben asked as he jingled his truck keys.

"I am and when I get there I'm going to soak in the hot tub." Larry opened the passenger-side door and before he got in he said, "Hope it's hot."

Jeff stared at him and didn't move to get in the vehicle. Larry waited and finally said, "I only met you a couple months ago, Jeff, but whatever you were going to say, say it."

"You're nuts, Lar. A hot tub? I've got one going on around the waist of my jeans. Not sure you want to join that party."

"The word picture you painted won't be leaving me for another decade or two. I think what you mean, there's a 'sauna' going on around your middle."

"Call it what you will and right now I'd change our name from Early Birds to Southern Fried Birds."

"Catchy name. We'll run it by our wives at the next meeting."

Larry and the other two laughed as they made their way to the RV Park. On the last leg of their travels, he settled back and took in the view of the ocean to their left. No longer a betting man, but he'd wager the clouds moving in guaranteed another sunset worth documenting.

When they landed, Larry forgot all about the hot tub and took his camera and lawn chair and walked across the street to the beach. He sat down and for the next hour, he snapped pictures of anything that caught his eye.

That was until a voice behind him said, "Dinner's ready." Larry almost jumped out of his chair at his wife's announcement and wanted to tell her to warn him of her arrival next time. Text him, or send up flares.

He stood and folded up his chair and as he walked over to join his wife at the picnic table she now occupied, Rosie said, "I wondered where you went."

"Wasn't too far from home," Larry commented as he put his camera up to his eye and took another shot of the fading colors of the evening's sunset.

"Can't wait to see your pictures, hon. Loved the last ones you took." Rosie patted his arm and continued, "Guess now you'll be taking them down in Florida. Don't know about you, but I'm sad to leave this place."

"Me too." Larry offered his wife his hand. "Shall we?"

"We shall."

***

"Will the Stevenson's, Wilford's & Miller's come up front." Pastor Steve said from the pulpit.

When Rose heard their names, she glanced at her choice of pink tee and dark blue capris. Not too bad for an oldie, but goodie. And her gray and florescent green tennis shoes added some pizazz to her outfit.

*Vogue, here I come.*

The Early Birds made their way to the front of the First Baptist Church. Jan Kendall, Linda and Steve greeted them with a round of hugs. While this went on, the congregation applauded.

Rose stood next to Larry. As she looked out at the crowd, she wanted to chuckle and nudge her friend in the rib and tell her, "Bets, we're truly celebs. We've made it on stage twice in one we—"

"God has done it again," Steve said. "With a few hands and servant hearts, He did amazing things in a short amount of time. These six people came in here and taught me how to do life. Thank you!"

"I have to add, the women taught me how to treat someone who's struggling to make it in this world." Jan stepped over to the piano and got a tissue, giving one out to everyone on the stage.

"I ditto what Jan said." Linda dabbed at her eyes.

Rose couldn't say a word if someone held her head in a vice. But plenty floated around in her head, wanting out. Only problem, them getting over the lump in her throat and not blubbering when she spoke.

She saw her hubby, usually Mr. Keep To Yourself, reach out for the mic. The pastor, wearing a smile and donning flip flops, handed it to him.

"I'm sure I speak for my friends when I say, 'No, thank you for having us. We had lots of fun.'"

Larry held the mic until Jeff reached for it and said, "We

105

weren't here as long, but Mary and I enjoyed ourselves. Reminds me of a story someone told me about the loaves and fishes. Bring a little and the Lord multiplies."

Ben took the microphone and it squawked. "That's why I don't use these things. Anyway, thanks everyone. If you didn't know it, you've got quite a pastor here. Hold on to him."

The congregation stood and cheered again. Rose clapped along then went down and hugged as many members of the church as possible before Pastor Steve told everyone to take their seat.

"After service we're giving tours of our new sanctuary, along with the Harvest Party. If anyone's interested. Can't wait to show off the workmanship the Lord blessed us with, but first let's dig into the word.

"The new series I'm starting today is called Gifts. The first point is: Gifts…The Ones You'd Rather Throw Away."

*He must mean slippers, underwear, or the flowered centerpiece from an older relative.*

Rose listened to Steve's message, then scanned the congregation to her right and left to make sure no one noticed how much she squirmed in her seat. She also checked to see if anyone else felt the pinch from the words the preacher delivered.

No one else appeared to find fault in anything he preached. However, Rosie wanted to contradict his definition of 'gifts' when he said, right from the pulpit, "It's those things you never ask for: fear, anxious thoughts, lack of faith."

Rose fumed while the preacher made his case, but when he brought health concerns into the mix and classified them as 'gifts', Larry almost had to hold her down. So much for the Harvest Festival that afternoon.

"Change your mind set. If you're dealing with anything I've talked about today, I ask you to see your circumstances differently. Instead of saying it's not the gift I wanted. Set your mind on things above. As in Colossians 3:2.

"Set it above the fear and anxious thoughts. Above the test results. Above the phone call. Ask the Lord to take your mind and heart away from the 'gifts' you didn't want and put them back on Him. He is our refuge and our strength."

Rose let his words settle over her. Peace replaced the urge she'd had to rush the stage and hurt the man preaching on it. Again a lump showed up in her throat, but this time she let it go and cried like a little bitty baby.

This after she realized her fear not only crippled her life, but Larry's too. Then a not-so-happy thought hit her as she sat there. One Rosie couldn't deny. She'd actually contributed to Larry's blood pressure problems each time she refused to drive their 5th wheel.

*Father, forgive me.*

"Let's bow our heads."

Rose's heart ached for her actions, but she also knew the Lord forgave the not-too-bright people out in the world. At that moment, she occupied the first chair of the world's biggest ding dongs.

"And all the people said, Amen!"

Rose wanted to hoot at the preacher's perfect timing, but instead she followed Larry and the rest of the Early Birds out of the church. While they stood chatting with some of the members, she told them, "Steve's a keeper. This was such an outstanding service."

She felt a tug on her arm and saw her hubby standing next to her. From the glint of laughter in his eyes and the mischievous grin on his face—Rose could only guess the words wanting to spill out of his mouth.

"Rosie, either you have ants in your pants or something in Steve's preaching got you riled. One things for sure, you burned some serious calories in there."

"I'm happy to report that no insects are housed in my pantaloons. But me and God, of course, we are working on my complete res-tor-a-tion."

Larry's laughter filled the foyer. After a minute he recovered and said, "Whatever it is, Rosie, keep at it. While you're rebuilding, Ben, Jeff and I will go to the truck to get the coolers? We'll meet you ladies outside."

Rosie heard her hubby's continued amusement all the way out the side door. No doubt he told the men his version of her squirminess. She'd have followed and corrected him, but decided to let the Lord continue the work in her. Even if it meant sewing her mouth shut in the process.

This interaction with the Almighty tickled her and a tiny snort followed. Rosie peeked around again to make sure her noise went unnoticed, but found Betsy heading in her direction with a smile on her face.

"I don't know what's going on with you, but I've seen about six different expressions on your face so far today." Betsy reached over and touched Rosie's forehead. "Then I catch you laughing over here all by yourself. I'm getting a little worried about you."

Rosie pushed her friend's hand away and said, "You worry too much. Must not be reading your "Do not Fear" verses I gave you?"

"The ones you gave me six-months ago. Don't need 'em, Rosie. I conquered my fears. Remember, I'm the one who drove the monstrosity."

"The Lord and I are working on it. Takes time."

"Smart thing to get Him involved."

"You're telling me. Now, why don't we go find the others?"

At the Harvest Party people asked them about their RV lifestyle. If she didn't answer the same question of, "How do you live in something so small?" fifty times, Rosie expounded on it seventy-five times.

Her response, "It's a gem to clean. Wished we'd done it sooner."

"Do you ever want a larger space to get away from each other?"

Rose left that pointed question to any of the other five. No need to elaborate on the lack of marital bliss at times when they'd spent too many 24/7s cooped up together. To her surprise, Larry popped off with an answer directly from heaven.

"There's no manual, and I wish there was, on how to get along in any size space. From my perspective—you learn to give it all to the Lord and whatever space you're in. That will always make it the perfect size."

Lots of ahs and 'Isn't that sweet' came from the women in the crowd. And her hubby's words almost caused Rosie's legs to give out from under her. When she steadied herself, she went over and planted a kiss on his cheek.

"Rose, you better hold onto him."

"That's my plan."

Rosie intended to hold on tight and make sure Larry knew he meant the world to her. In their tiny home on wheels, their place in

Texas, or standing on the lawn of the First Baptist Church on a Sunday afternoon.

*Lord, You've given me a gift in Mr. Larry Wilford. He's one I'll definitely keep.*

## CHAPTER THIRTEEN

On Monday morning Larry, with Baby in tow, made a visit to Ben's trailer after the ladies went to church again. He knocked on the screen and heard a "come in" from inside.

Larry carried Baby up the steps and put her down at the door. Matilda greeted him with her usual jumping-around routine. At one point she jumped so high, he caught her in mid-air and held her.

"My dog's got your attention, what can I do for you?"

Larry wanted to ask his friend if he saw the same thing he'd seen on Sunday, concerning Rosie. But he didn't know how to say it without sounding like he'd become the one diagnosing someone else. Normally his wife's job.

"I repeat, what's going on. Other than you standing next to my front door, holding my dog. Baby is starting to stare at you."

"She's admiring my haircut. Trimmed it this morning." Larry put Matilda down and took a mug off the counter and filled it with coffee.

"Will you sit down and tell me what's going on. Your stalling is killing me and the pooches."

"I'm not one to analyze anyone's behavior, my wife included.

But after yesterday's sermon and how she acted last night. Rosie's blaming herself for everything wrong with me, including my high blood pressure."

"Funny you should mention that." Ben stirred some cream into his coffee. "Bets said she thought something happened to Rose and was going to ask her about it today."

"Ben, she about drove me bonkers after we got home. Fussing. You know I don't do fussing. Not at all."

"She's always fussing over you, be it diagnosing you or telling you how you chew your food."

"You're right about that, but this time it was different."

"I'm sure she'll talk to Betsy and Mary. Girlfriends save lots of marriages and cure what troubles them. It'll be fine."

"I hope so. Got another question, since we're free from interruptions, do you want to go look at RVs?"

"I'm ready to go shopping whenever you are," Jeff's voice sounded from outside.

"Were you eavesdropping on us?"

"No, just walking by."

"Come on in."

"How about I stay out here and wait. Sounded like you were ready to go somewhere."

"We are."

Ben followed Larry down the stairs and after he told Matilda to behave and handed Baby to Larry he said, "Jeff, you want to drive? I've never ridden in a P.T. Cruiser before."

"Me neither. Be sure to put the top down while I'm taking the pooch home."

"Guess I'm driving." Jeff got his keys out of his pocket.

A minute later Larry got in the back seat and put the dealership's address in his phone. A British-sounding voice guided them to I-10. Even though the calendar read the end of October, the warm air felt wonderful.

Life didn't get any better than in a convertible. A smile broke out on Larry's face and he rationalized—if he traded in the 5th wheel and truck, they could buy a convertible as their tow car then drive it to the beach.

*I'm liking it.*

Jeff parked in front of the dealership and everyone piled out of the car. Larry's daydreaming of a convertible would have to wait. Today he wanted to look at Class C motorhomes to get an idea what the smaller units had to offer. Try to imagine themselves living inside of the smaller space, with their dog underfoot.

*Cozy, for sure. Am I nuts?*

A suntanned fellow approached and said, "Hi, I'm Ken. May I help you?"

"Hope so. I'd like to see your Class Cs."

"Lar, if you wanted to see inside one of them, why not look at ours?"

"Sir, you own one of these?"

Jeff straightened to his full height and said, "I sure do."

"How?"

Larry appreciated the salesman's question. Same one he'd wanted to ask since Jeff and Mary came to the RV park with their new rig.

"Once I get in the door, it's smooth sailing. Ceilings are plenty tall enough and the bed, it's a super queen. For the rest, and you know what I mean, I use the RV Park's facilities. Now, back to my question. Larry, why didn't you look at our RV?"

"I wanted to see one without anything in it."

"Makes sense. I do have one complaint on the one we bought and suggest you not buy the one with the lighter flooring." Jeff shook his head "no" for emphasis. "Every speck of dust shows on it. Glad we never got a dog."

"You're missing out, but I'm not making the final decision this morning. Rosie will need to see it and approve it all before anything happens. Also, Ken, before we go any further—do you take a trade in of a 2012 5th wheel and a dually truck?"

"Did one of those last week. I'm sure we'd trade on another one. As long as it's in good shape. Can I go out and look at it?"

"Don't have it with us, but can bring it out at a later date."

"No problem. How about we go check some out?"

Larry and Ken walked into the large showroom at Majestic RV. Every kind of trailer, 5th wheel, Class A and C sat in the expansive warehouse. Some had their awning out and doors open, inviting visitors to come inside the unit.

As they approached a Class A, the salesman said, "What about this one?"

"I'd go with something like this, but don't want the length anymore. I'm an accident waiting to happen."

He went on to tell Ken about the picnic table incident and the time he got too close to the light pole. "But, not to worry, I'll get them fixed before we trade them in. Be as good as new."

"Larry, we've seen it all. One gentleman's compartment door hung on by a thread when he brought his 5er in. We took in the trade, minus some money for the damage, but what I told him— we're only human. Can't be mad at ourselves for a bump here and there."

"When you're with two other couples, and they're watching your every move, backing in takes on a whole new meaning. Those guys like to harass me. There will come a day when one of them does something and I'll try not to badger them too much."

"Sounds like they'd deserve some harassment."

"They would, but I'd try to keep it to a minimum." Larry chuckled. "And pray like mad, hoping the Lord held my tongue."

This time Ken laughed. "He's held mine plenty of times and I've been grateful. How about we look around at some of the Class Cs and you can decide on the ones you like? Then we can sit down and talk some numbers?"

The four toured a dozen motorhomes. Every design known to man. Ken pointed out the features and what he liked about the coaches. Larry appreciated the input and said, "Not sure I'll remember a single thing you've told us, but I appreciate it."

"We've got brochures. I'll make sure I send you home with all of them."

"I've been to RV shows, Ken. Will you give me a bag to carry them in, too?"

"It's the way we fly. How about we go in and crunch some numbers."

"You guys go entertain yourselves. We won't be too long. Will we, Ken?"

"He'll be out in no time."

Larry watched Ken once they went to his office. He took papers out of a file drawer and lined them in front of him on the desk. He asked him questions about their truck and trailer. How he'd rate the wear and tear on each. In the end he gave Larry a price.

"Did I hear you right? You haven't even seen our RV."

"I trust what you told me and I'm pretty good at reading people. You leveled with me about how you tried to take the side and back end off your trailer." Ken smiled.

"I call them almost near misses. And I'm hoping with the smaller unit I'll have less chance of—"

"Backing into a picnic table."

"Ben, we were doing fine without you."

"Thought you needed some help."

"I think we're done. Ken, give me one of your cards and I'll be in touch."

"Looking forward to doing business with you."

They shook Ken's hand and went to find Jeff. All the while the two walked, Larry kept thinking about the price Ken quoted him. They found Jeff lounging in a lawn chair under one of the RV awnings, drinking water.

"Did you sign on the dotted line?"

"No I didn't, Jeff, but it was tempting."

"If you'd been much longer, I was going to go into one of the 5th wheels and turn on the A/C." Jeff took the flyer and fanned himself.

"You poor thing. You won't melt. How about we get going and let the tropical breezes cool us off?" Larry got in the back seat and again the convertible grabbed his full attention and he decided trading in the RV and truck would work out just fine.

As Jeff drove toward the campground, Larry told them about the deal Majestic RV offered him. "I can't believe it and it was sight unseen."

"Lar, that is pretty amazing," Ben said as he glanced in the back seat.

"Guys, there's another thing, we have to keep this outing to ourselves, so I can talk to Rose about it. Don't want it to be a group discussion when I suggest we move to an even smaller RV. I can hear her now, 'What will we do with all the stuff in the 5th wheel?'"

"She'll say that and more. I'd think you'd want the Early Birds there for moral support?" Ben smiled.

"This is the best way. If I come out of the 5th wheel bruised and bloody, that's when you two can intervene. Not before."

"Count on us to keep quiet."

"Lar, I'll take the bag of brochures Ken gave you. Don't want Rosie to find those either."

"I'd forgotten about them."

Jeff pulled the car in and parked. Larry waited for Ben to push the front seat forward to make it easier to get out. Once they accomplished that, they settled into their chairs as if they'd been lounging there all day. No one would know they'd only returned five minutes before.

Unless someone bumped their arm against the front of the car, which his wife did with her usual flair and announced to everyone, "Where'd you gentlemen go. Thought you were staying here, batting down the hatches for when we leave day after tomorrow."

*Why? Lord, I ask, why does she have to...*

Larry left his thought dangling and hung his head. No keeping their trip from Rosebud. Blood or no blood in the end.

His wife crossed her arms—her usual stance when she waited for an answer to her question. He delayed saying anything while he watched his allies, the other Early Birds, scatter as if a fire drill sounded and they had to find an open fire hydrant.

Larry chuckled, but Rosie's tight-lipped expression and continued closed stance made him swallow any witty comeback churning inside of him.

"Okay, mister, since everyone left us. Tell me what's going on."

"I'm not sure what happened, other than someone, Ben, must have texted Betsy for everyone to hunker down in a safe place."

Larry laughed until tears ran down his cheeks, but his wife's joyousness—nary a hint of happiness anywhere. No snorts or snickers coming from Rosie's direction.

"Why would our friends need to hunker down...my love?"

"Rosie, come over here and sit down." Larry opened one of the folding chairs and sat it next to his.

She hesitated.

"Come on, hon."

"Don't try and butter me up."

"If I was going to do that, I'd offer you some of Betsy's potato salad."

"That sounds good, but I'd rather hear what you have to say."

*I'm sure you would. Help, Lord!*

Larry wanted to stall for more time, hoping the Lord answered him. Or send his friends outside again to help him. But they'd done exactly what he'd asked them to do.

"Are you going to tell me today?" Rose took a drink out of the water bottle she held in her right hand.

Larry leaned forward in his chair and took Rosie's other hand. "Sweetie, how would you like to go look at one of those Class C motorhomes? Like Jeff and Mary's? See if we'd like to own one?"

"I'm not sure if I should kill you or kiss you."

"I opt for the kissing. A much better plan." Larry smiled, hoping his wife tended toward the latter too.

"You would, old man. That's what you three did today, wasn't it? Planning my future without consulting me first."

"Yep. How am I doing?"

Rose hopped out of the chair and almost mowed him down when she hugged him around the neck.

*Yes, I think she likes my idea.*

"So, you're not going to kill me?"

"Heavens no. That's the most brilliant decision you've made since you married me forty-seven years ago."

"Then I'm a 'gift' you're going to keep?"

"Funny you should mention 'Gifts'." Rose sat down next to him again. "The sermon yesterday sort of ties in with your suggestion to downsize. You know, getting rid of things."

"Steve's talk sure had you wriggling all over the place."

"You noticed."

"Dear, you kept bumping into me. For once it wasn't you poking me in my ribs to hear what the preacher said."

"No, the Lord poked me plenty about your—"

"Rosie, you are not responsible for anything to do with my blood pressure. Not helping me drive didn't cause it. Stress and too many close calls with the 5th wheel did. The sucker is way too big for my liking anymore."

"And, Lar, if we get a smaller one, I can help you drive. No more bugging me to take over when you're tired. I'll take the wheel with a smile on my face. Oh, that is when you've given me some lessons."

If he hadn't been sitting, Larry would have fainted from his wife's willingness to learn to drive.

*Am I dreaming?*

"Is it safe to come out?"

Ben's question stopped the high-spirited party inside Larry's head and he said, "Come on out. It's safe and I'm shocked at how well Rosie handled the news. Wonders will never cease."

"She said more than that." Rose poked Larry. "She also said she'd be willing to drive the smaller thing. So, when is the happy couple, us, going to go RV shopping?"

"First, before I answer that, I need to find out something else. Why is it when I think you'll be mad, you're not? Then the next time, you're fuming when I thought you wouldn't say a word?"

"It's simple. I want to keep you on your toes. Always guessing what might happen next." Rose snorted.

"Should of known."

Ben sat in one of the chairs and turned toward Larry. "Bud, it's a woman thing. I know I'm married to one of those special species."

"I'd say you'd be wise not to call Betsy, or me, a living organism."

"Rosie, you do take things so literal."

"I do. That's what makes me so unique. Anyway, Larry, when *are* we going to check out our new home?"

He stared at his wife, still not believing she'd gone along with his latest idea. Before she changed her mind he said, "Is tomorrow too soon?"

CHAPTER FOURTEEN

While Rose waited for Larry to pick her up at Sassy Seconds the next day, she hung clothes on hangers. All morning her mind went from almost jumping out of her skin with excitement, to the thought they'd fallen into the nut wagon wanting to switch RVs.

However, the idea of a cute Class C excited her. She'd had her eye on one when they'd purchased the 5th wheel four years before and tried to convince Larry of the smaller unit then, but nooooooooooo!

"Hon, it's exactly what we need."

"I'm telling you, Rosie, you'd never like it."

"How do you know?"

"I know you. The more space you have, the better it is for all of us."

"But it's adorable."

"Adorable and less than 140 square feet."

Rosie covered her mouth to muffle her words and said, "It's still adorable."

"I heard you, but is it sensible?"

In the end Rose swayed to Larry's side and they bought the monstrosity. For the most part they'd enjoyed traveling in the larger-than-life trailer. Especially when they stopped for longer periods of time.

*Like Colorado and Biloxi. Kind of nice to have the room when we're in one spot.*

With that reasoning, Rose decided they'd keep the 5th wheel. They had too much stuff. What would they do with it? She sure didn't want to rent a trailer to haul behind their new rig. A car belonged back there.

For some reason, this thought made her laugh out loud. And since no one kept her company in the back room of Sassy Seconds, she had a pretty good chuckle at the image of their access baggage trailing behind them. That was until someone cleared their throat.

Rosie glanced in the direction the noise came from and saw Betsy walking toward her. When her friend stood next to her, she said, "I'm not sure what's going on with you, but your expressions today should have been taped and put to music. No doubt, they'd be big winners at the Sundance Film Festival."

"If it guaranteed I'd meet Robert Redford, I'd let you tape me doing most anything. Another thing, I'd hope Mr. Redford would help me quit waffling on the decision to downsize. For that, I'd do it for sure."

"No, my dear friend, this one's all you and Larry's. Bob won't have anything to say about the switch."

"I need someone to help."

"Whatever you decide, I'm sure your hubby has prayed about the decision, leaving nothing to chance."

"I'm sure he has. I spent half the night wrestling with the Lord on the pros and cons of it after Larry told me. Initially I said I wanted to do it, but now I'm not so sure."

"Remember how tentative I was a year ago, concerning the RV lifestyle. You've done it for a long time and know what you want. The smaller unit is the ticket for the two of you."

"Bets, I don't say this often enough, but I love you and you're my voice of reason in times of trouble."

"Most of the time."

"All the time. We're making the move and that's my final answer." Rose laughed. Happy to have made the decision.

"Got another question for you, Rosie. Don't know if you've thought about it, but where are you going to put the plaque in your new place?"

In all honesty, the sign or the placement of it hadn't crossed

Rose's mind. What she remembered from their previous perusal of Class Cs, the wall space consisted of a small spot next to the refrigerator and the open area above the cab of the truck.

"I said I loved you, but I'm reconsidering my adoration for you after your insensitive comment, Betsy."

"Insensitive? Never."

"Guess I'll hang the plaque on the back of your RV so I can see it while we're going down the road."

"That means that we'll always lead the way."

"The way Larry drives—that could be a good thing."

Rose heard a gasp from Bets and the back door slam shut. She glanced to her left and saw her hubby. The scowl on his face told her he'd heard her not-so-kind comment. But what he said next, solidified he'd heard every word she said.

"Here are the keys. You can drive the truck since I'm so inept."

"Think it's time for me to help in the front." Betsy scurried toward the curtain and disappeared behind it.

"I'm sorry." And she meant every word.

"Rosie, if I didn't love you so much, I'd trade you in on another model."

"Is that right, Mr. Wilford? I am pretty sure you'd get a pretty penny out of me if you did. I've got some features that don't come standard anymore."

"That you do, my dear. We'd cash in the mother lode on your sense of humor alone."

"So glad you get that about me."

"Oh, I get something, Rosie, but I'm not sure what."

"On that note, are you ready to go? I'll drive if you want me to." Rose reached out to take his keys.

"Ain't happening. Don't want to take any chances at more damage."

"Are you sure?" Rose gave Larry a peck on the cheek. "Hey, I've got a better idea. Call the salesman. Tell him to send someone to drive it the rest of the way. You can't be trusted either. The picnic table in Baton Rouge is still talking about your encounter with it."

Rose's laughter rang out and Larry joined in with the hilarity. She grabbed her fanny pack and as she headed to the truck she shouted, "Let's get this show on the road."

***

"Larry, GPS told you to turn here."

"No, it's the next driveway. More room for the truck and RV."

He pulled in and when he went over and opened his wife's door he said, "I'm within the lines. On both sides."

"Practice makes perfect. As they say."

"I'll be saying the same about you in a few days. You've been driving the dually truck, without the monster, so you'll do fine driving the Class C. It's a smidge longer than the truck, but not by much." Larry extended his thumb and index finger.

"Your measurement is off a few feet, Lar, but thanks for the encouragement. I'll need it when I do get behind the wheel of one of those."

Larry turned to where Rosie pointed. A row of Class Cs, all different sizes, sat to the left of where they parked. Again, their doors open, beckoning anyone visiting to take a look inside.

Along with the Cs, he also noticed three Class A motorhomes in the mix. This took Larry back a little. He'd told Ken they wanted Class Cs and no more than a twenty-seven footer. Nothing too big.

"I know what you're thinking, Larry," Ken said as he came out of the first Class C.

"You're killing me." Larry shook his head then continued, "Go close the doors on the big rigs before Rosie runs over to one of them and falls in love."

"Hi, I'm Rose. Nice to meet you and there's no need to shut any doors. I've got self-control."

Ken laughed. "I'm sure you do. Larry's the one who worries me. From the size of your 5th wheel, bigger is better."

"Not in our case. Smaller is superior."

"Rosie, why don't you take a look around. See what hits you, but keep it under twenty-seven foot. Okay?"

"Sure thing, sugar."

After his wife walked away Larry and Ken talked. Again the salesman reminded him, "You do know you'll have a lot less space."

"I can live with less. Rose, I'm not so sure."

"Larry, get in here. I love it. I'm ready to make a de…" Rose

121

stopped talking and stared off in the distance.

He turned to see what stopped his wife from speaking and said, "Betsy, what are you doing here? And you brought everyone with you?"

"Sure did and we're here to approve of your purchase." Betsy hugged Rose when she got over to her.

"You do have an interesting group of friends."

"Ken, the Early Birds stick together. Through thick and thin. High blood pressure and—"

"He gets the idea, Rosie."

"Fine. Come on Bets. Mary. Come see our new home."

The women disappeared inside what Rose called 'their new home'. He decided he better go and see what he'd traded in his truck and RV for before she signed the papers.

*Lord, calm my...our hearts. Help us both make the best decision.*

While he prayed, Larry watched Betsy and Mary leave the RV, chattering amongst themselves. Rose stuck her head out of the door and said, "The ladies approve. You better come and check it out, or is it all my decision?"

Larry walked inside and asked, "Did you check the price?"

"No." Rose picked up the MSRP sheet and waved it in the air. "Hon, I don't understand a thing about the engine, but the décor. I'm lovin' it. Lookie here. I can accent the daylights out of this place with beachy material on the pillows. A turquoise blanket, it'd set the tone for the bed." She stopped then said, "What are you laughing at?"

"You. Did you pay attention to anything else? Storage? Drawer space?"

"No. No and no."

"Where are you going to put your toaster?" Your shoes? Clothes? How about your laundry basket?"

Larry watched his wife. She took a seat at the built-in banquette and her eyes filled and before her wail reached clear to Jackson, Mississippi, Larry hurried over to her. "I'm sorry, but we need to make sure this will fit what we need. Not what we 'want'."

"You're right." Rose wiped her eyes. "Can we walk around and pretend we're putting our things away?"

"Let's start in the bathroom."

Larry walked the short distance and motioned Rose to follow. The two squeezed in the tiny room then he reached in front of his wife and opened the corner cabinet. He tried to envision their toiletries in it. The small lip on the front gave him an idea.

"The first thing I'd do is silicone a piece of Plexiglas across the front of each shelf. That way items won't fall out."

"That will work."

"Now you'll need to step out for me to check under the sink. Too tight in here for that maneuver."

Rosie complied and while she leaned on him to look herself, Larry peered inside the compact area. He decided whatever cleaning products they used in the other RV, they'd fit in there too.

Next on the agenda: the shower.

"Hon, since we use the facilities at the park more than our own, I can assume we'd continue doing the same. We'll use the shower as our closet. That way it stays clean and it can be our hamper too. Even store the extra water we buy."

Rose stood on her tiptoes and kissed him. When she stepped back she said, "Lar, we don't need to worry about buying this. There's plenty of room. Anyway, it says in the Bible we're not supposed to fret about anything."

"But it tells us not to rush into anything either."

"Where does it say that?" Rose smiled.

"Somewhere between the Declaration of Independence and the Night Before Christmas. You know what I mean."

"You were scaring me for a moment. And by the sounds of it—you need to get into your Bible and do some studying."

For the next fifteen minutes Larry and Rose opened and closed every door inside the Class C. If he didn't say what would go in one cabinet or drawer, his wife filled it with their clothes or food items.

The way Rosie organized, as in their 5th wheel, they'd have enough room. Larry's shoulders relaxed and he enjoyed their brainstorming session through their supposed 'new home'.

His excitement grew more when he looked closer at the outside compartments. Their size eased his mind. A bit. Yes, they paled in comparison to their monster, but the manufacturer of the unit made good use of every inch of the underneath.

Larry went back inside and could tell his wife, in her own

mind, had already placed their belongings inside the nooks and crannies of the Class C motorhome. It looked like they'd be living in a MUCH smaller space. With an occasional yappy pooch.

*Glory be!*

"I'm ready if you are?" Larry reached to take Rose's hand.

"Me, too."

Larry glanced outside to find Ken and said the magic words any salesman wanted to hear, "We'll take it."

"Let me show you a few things first."

Ken came inside and hit a button near the front door and the awning came out. A light easterly breeze caught it and made it flutter. But when the salesman went out to tighten the screws on each side, it didn't bounce as much.

"There's lots of reasons to buy this unit, but the awning tops the list."

"Personally, I'm partial to the size. What did Larry say, "Smaller is superior? Swish. Swish. Swish. The floor of my teeny tiny bathroom is clean.""

"Only Rosie would share that with the world."

"That's why we love her. Are you going to do it?" Mary stood next to the RV.

"Yep." Larry stepped out of the Class C. "Why don't you guys go back to the park and tell them a new unit is coming in."

"While we're at it, want us to bring you boxes to move from your fiver to this one?" Jeff asked. "You do need to do it before you can move this one to the RV Park."

"Guess neither of us thought that far. Yes, we'd appreciate it if you'd grab some boxes and give us a hand later."

"Will do."

"I'll be inside when you two are ready to sign the papers." Ken headed toward the dealership.

*Moving day.*

Larry's thought went by the wayside when he saw his wife rush back into the motor home.

*She's changed her mind. I knew it.*

He hurried into the Class C and watched Rosie as she moved her head from side to side, as if she'd lost something. Fifteen seconds into her search, he asked her, "What in the world are you looking for?"

"I'm not looking for anything. I want to know where I'm going to put it?"

"Hon, please relax and tell me what we need to put where."

Rose told him about the plaque she'd bought from Sassy Seconds. "Come here. I'll show it to you."

The minute Rose took the sign out of the back of the truck, he remembered seeing it and said, "We'll find a spot for it."

*Not sure where, but I'll move heaven and earth…*

Larry took his wife's hand and they walked back inside. He pointed above the cab of the truck. "This spot will work. A couple strips of Velcro on the wall and on the back of the plaque. It'll stay there for us to enjoy for years to come."

Rose put her arms around him and gave him another kiss. This one a doozer. When she stepped away she said, "I never had a doubt you'd figure it out. That's why I love you so much. Let's go sign the papers and get moving."

CHAPTER FIFTEEN

Rose made another trip between the two RVs, dodging two of the Early Birds who piled boxes outside the door of the Class C. Every ounce of her wanted to sit on the pavement and yell, "Quit already. Too much stuff," but she kept quiet.

"This is the last box." Ben announced.

"Glory to God in the Highest."

"Can't talk Christmas until after Thanksgiving, Rosie."

"Bets, I'm praising my Savior for..." Rose tried to name one thing she was thankful for, but all the wonders of their months on the road bombarded her brain at the same time, so she said, "Too many blessings to count. One thing though, I'm asking Him to give me a little more space in our new abode."

"What's the problem. You only lost ten feet of space." Jeff laughed.

"If I wasn't a Christian and a dignified woman at a place of business I'd come over there and clobber you."

"Watch out or Ben will find a biblical story to go along with what you're saying."

Ben sat the box he was carrying on top of the stack and said, "Wish I had something, but I'm with Rosie, you need more room. This pup's about ready to burst at the seams."

"See, I told you."

"Rosie, quit pestering these people and keep stuffing."

"For your information, you old poop, I'm not stuffing anything anywhere."

"I am," Betsy's voice rang out.

After their laughter died down, Rosie decided to bring up the dreaded "S" word. Storage. Since no one else mentioned it, she'd be the first. From the stack of boxes sitting next to their doorstep, they'd be picking out a unit the following day.

"Rose, do you want me to hand you this kitchen box?"

"No, I think it's time we stopped and regrouped." Rosie sat down on the bottom step of their new RV and waited for the rest of the Early Birds to join her there.

They stopped and gathered around and Rosie decided the only thing missing in the parking lot of Majestic RV was the fire pit and someone roasting marshmallows. This imagery made her chuckle, which caused Larry to glance her way and ask, "Are you okay, hon?"

"I'm fine, but the new RV's groaning. Can you hear it?"

"I hear it saying, 'Storage. We need storage.'"

"Exactly, Lar. I say we load the boxes inside, wherever they fit. Tomorrow we can find a 5x5 storage unit to put them in."

"I've got an even better idea." Betsy took one of the boxes and went to the back of their truck. "We'll put the boxes in here and take them to Florida for you. That way you're not scattered over all of God's country."

"Then you'll be able to go through the boxes once you're settled down there. Hey, maybe there's another second-hand store you can donate the items you don't need anymore."

"I'm liken' the idea of giving more stuff away, but I'll guarantee whatever store we find won't measure up to Sassy Seconds." Rose stopped then added, "Unless we get a hold of it."

"Rosie, right now I'd love to hold a taco." Ben held his hands up to his mouth and pretended to take a bite.

"Taco Bell it is and Larry is leading the way with his new ride."

"No, Jeff, my man. It's Rosie's turn." Larry put his arm around his wife's shoulder and said, "Ken gave you a set of keys. How about you drive her home?"

Rose's chubby knees began to shake like Jell-O not yet set

and her long-forgotten symptoms of IBS gave a shout out in a mighty way.

"Lar, since it's getting close to dark, why don't you drive? Rose can practice some other time. What do you say?"

Rose didn't wait for her hubby to answer Ben's question. She went over and hopped into the passenger seat of their new Class C and made a plan. When they returned to the RV Park, she'd give Ben a kiss for saving her and Lar's life from certain doom, if she'd taken the wheel.

*I-10 isn't ready for the likes of me. Yet. Not until...*

Larry jumped in and without a word took off on the major highway, which led to their favorite restaurant. His smile reassured her he'd live through her not driving. Again. But this time her not taking the wheel gnawed on her.

The one note she'd written down on Sunday came to mind. *F.E.A.R. False Expectations Appearing Real.*

"Which is a big, fat lie."

Rosie glanced over at her hubby to see if he'd heard her outburst. Apparently he hadn't. Driving their new purchase took all of his attention. His eyes stayed straight ahead and he held the steering wheel tight, locked in the ten and two configuration.

*If I poked him right now—he'd make us a sunroof.*

She chuckled and decided to leave well enough alone. Didn't want any modifications to their unit on its maiden voyage. Rose's phone buzzed and she looked down and saw a picture of Everly and daughter in the right corner of the screen.

When she hit the button the text said, "Won't be in Sassy Seconds in the a.m. Will call you later."

"I hope we get to see her before we go."

"See who?"

"Everly. She's not coming in tomorrow."

"To the RV Park?"

"No. To church." Rose swatted his arm. "Do you even know who Everly is?"

"She's one of the ladies you helped at the church."

"I'm impressed."

"You should be. Don't you need to text her back?"

Rose laughed at her husband. The man who acted like he didn't pay a lick of attention. Then in the next breath, he'd tell you, with the exact words, what you'd said three days before. What a guy.

Rose texted Everly, "I hope we get to see you before we leave."

Again her phone buzzed and words on the screen almost made Rosie cry. "I hope so. ☹

When she put her phone down on her lap, Rose babbled on about Everly and Douglas. "They're such a cute couple. I can see the two of them together. The other thing, Olivia needs a dad in her life. I remember when I was sixteen."

"You can remember that far back?" Larry took a quick look at his wife then turned his attention back on the road and said, "Anyway, dear, when did you become a matchmaker? Thought you only diagnosed people's supposed diseases."

"Larry, I remember a whole bunch of things and I'll always diagnose. It's my gift. But when I saw those two together, they're a match made in heaven. Unlike someone else I know. However, if you play your cards right, you'll make it to another anniversary. Not working so well with those kinds of comments."

"Couldn't resist."

"Try harder next time." Rose smiled and grabbed her phone. "I need to text Bets and Mary and tell them to pray about whatever is going on with Everly."

"You're going to see them in about three minutes."

"Never you mind." Rose messaged them and they answered within seconds. Both agreed to pray.

For some reason, planning a wedding flitted through Rose's mind. Not her fears. For that she smiled. And as Larry pulled into the parking lot, she prayed for a new beginning for Everly, Olivia and Douglas. At the end she added one of her own.

*Father, help me keep my eyes on You. Not on things external. Like navigating big rigs.*

\*\*\*

"We're home."

Rosie jumped out of the coach, but Larry stayed put. He wanted to stay and marvel at the size and ease of mobility of their new coach. He'd still need to watch where he backed it, even with the camera, but this RV appeared so much easier to handle than the 5er.

If his wife wouldn't have him hauled away, he'd almost kiss—"

"Say what?"

Rose had Larry's full attention. Off in the distance he saw his wife doing what he said he'd do a moment before. Kissing, but not their RV. Her lips graced Ben's cheek. From the look on his face, it surprised his friend as much as it did him.

Larry strolled over to them, but before he uttered a word, Rose grabbed his arm and said, "Nothing to worry about, dear, I'm repaying a debt of gratitude."

"By kissing Ben?"

"He kept us from a catastrophe. Or I should say, Ben saved our RV from me and my driving…on a cold, dreary starless night like tonight."

"Rosebud, if you get any more dramatic, I'm taking you to Broadway. I'm sure they need someone of your caliber who embellishes everything they think, say or do. And I mean ev…er…y…thing."

"Our trip to the Big Apple will have to wait until after we leave Florida. Hey, that's an idea. The Early Birds can go up the East Coast after we leave Ft. Myers. What do you say about that gang?"

"Why don't we get to Florida and discuss it down there?"

***

Two days later that's exactly what they did. At least the heading to Florida part. The six of them got on the road again with Jeff leading the way this time.

"Breaker 21. Can you read me?"

"Loud and clear, Ben. What's—"

"Betsy wants to sing the song."

"Oh no she doesn't." Larry's voice rang out.

"Yes, she does." Betsy answered.

"Sing it to Matilda. She loves the song. Wilford's signing off now." Larry put the mic back in its holder and laughed at his wittiness.

It became obvious his wife found his humor less than stellar and said, "Larry, you get on that contraption and say you're sorry."

"Bets will make us sing."

"It won't kill you."

"The apology or singing."

"Both."

"Oh alright."

In the end Betsy didn't make them sing and said, "Lar, Matilda appreciated being serenaded. Not sure if I appreciated when she covered her ears."

"There you go."

Larry signed off and put his full attention on driving I-10 and his wife jabbering about Everly's big news she'd shared with the women before they left.

"I cannot believe she's moving to Tampa, Florida. Only a little over two hours away from us."

"What about Douglas? Is he coming too?"

"That's the part of the story we didn't get into."

"Why's that?"

"She didn't seem to want to talk about it."

"Rose, you need to leave it alone then."

"Oh, I'm leaving it alone. Yeppers! That's what I'm doing."

Larry thought he heard one of her famous snorts, but let it go. Whatever his wife and the other two plotted, he'd hear about it later. He hoped he wouldn't read about it in the newspaper first.

The headline caption—*Sixty Plus Retirees Abducted in Matchmaking Scheme. Three women held without bond.*

"I'd suggest you tell me what's going on inside your head since your driving has taken on my tendencies. Slower than molasses in the wintertime."

"You don't want to know."

"Oh, yes I do. When it has something to do with me, I'm all ears."

Larry filled her in on the possible headline. His wife got as big of a kick out of it and took it a step further when she said, "Gray-haired Matchmakers Take Florida by Storm. 'No pun intended.'"

"What are you taking by storm? Everly and Douglas?"

"No, silly. When we find a building and franchise Sassy Seconds. I can see it now. With Linda's help, we'll take this nationwide. And since we're on the road, it can happen."

"Woman, I'd love to have your imagination. But it would hurt too much."

"It does, but that's why they invented aspirin."

Larry laughed and Rosie's mention of pills reminded him he hadn't taken his that morning. Once they landed in Tallahassee he'd take it. He'd also call the number Betsy's mom texted him to make an appointment to check on his blood pressure.

Along with that, he'd ask for a recommendation for a nutritionist. What better place to start than Florida to get into shape? No excuse not to exercise when temperatures stayed between warm to hot 365 days a year.

While the women planned someone's love life, the guys could ride their bikes and contact the pastor of the church in Ft. Myers. See what they needed done for the next three to four months.

The CB squawked, interrupting Larry's thoughts. Jeff's voice sounded, "In less than five miles, we'll take the exit for the state capital. The RV Park is two miles down on the left."

"I'll be shutting up then," Rose announced.

"That's right. If I hear a peep out of you, I'll put you and Baby on the next plane back to Houston."

"You'd do no such—"

Baby's barking and the crackle of the CB stopped their bantering. Larry hushed their pooch and listened to more instructions from Jeff. In less than fifteen minutes they parked their RVs and stood outside in the warmth of the afternoon sun. Their first stop in Florida.

Larry saw that their day held promise for them. A Taco Bell sat across the street. He could almost write the script of what would come next. Ben didn't surprise him when he said, "Anyone else hungry?"

"Again. We had it last night. I'll never get what all the excitement is about the place."

"Jeff, if you want to stay part of this group, don't question Benjamin and what he and Bets love to eat. They're easier to live with if you don't."

"Kind of like Jeff and Italian food." Mary put her arm around her husband's back. "Don't butt in line in front of him when there's pizza around."

"Is that why I ended up with a black eye when we worked together in Boulder."

Larry laughed and said, "I don't remember that."

"Okay, I fibbed a little." Ben stepped toward the street and said, "I'll race you. Whoever gets there last, pays."

Larry grabbed Rose's hand and they made a beeline to the side street, but the younger ones beat them. He'd pay for dinner. His diet and exercise program, they'd come at a later date.

## CHAPTER SIXTEEN

"Where do you think you're going in the heat of the day?" Rose glanced at Larry while he tied the laces of his tennis shoes.

"After last night's tacos, I'm going for a long walk."

"Take your dog, she needs some exercise too."

"Baby, you want to come along with Chubby." Larry laughed as he took her leash off the hook.

"Why don't you invite Ben and Jeff? Physical activity needs to knock on their door too." Rosie made a wide motion around her middle. "Then I'll head over and harass Betsy about her writing. I'm still waiting for the blog she promised the world."

"See you sometime."

Larry walked out the door and Rose texted Bets. A minute later she answered her ringing phone, "May I help you?"

"Rosie, you're never going to believe what happened. While searching on the computer, I found out the Lord moonlights for Google."

"I've heard He works in mysterious ways, but I'm not so sure He's got a second job at the search giant. Sit down, I'll be right there."

Rose hurried over, thinking Betsy had hit her head, after her last statement. And the babbling going on when she hit the top step of her friend's RV didn't change her mind. No word in the English language matched what Bets proclaimed, so Rosie asked, "NaanuWHAT?"

"NaNoWriMo."

"Oh that cleared it up. Are you studying a foreign language instead of writing?"

"It's not another language. It's National Novel Writing Month and it officially starts tomorrow. November first. I'm going to write my novel in thirty days."

"Good for you, but how is that possible?"

"I don't know, but I ordered Chris Baty's e-book, *No Plot? No Problem!* I've already read three chapters. I'm ready to hit the road writing."

"Girl, I haven't seen you this excited since we saw Willie Nelson."

"And with his song in the background while I'm writing, I can't go wrong. 50,000 words—here I come."

"Where do we begin?" Rose asked as she sat down at Betsy's table.

She glanced around for a pad of paper to document their continued brainstorming ideas, but no notepad sat around.

"Betsy, I'm going to climb out on a limb here and say most writers, which you are one of them, usually have something to write on. Where would I find such item?"

"You won't need anything to write on, Rosie. The only brainstorming going on will be between me and the Lord this time." Betsy reached across the table and took her hand. "I do hope you'll help me on a couple of other things…if you're interested."

"Glad I'm not pushed out of everything." Rose smiled then said, "Whatever you need, Bets, I'm at your service."

"I want you to pray like you've never prayed before. After that, please badger, harass and/or pester me. Pick one of the latter, but make me accountable each and every day. The book I'm reading makes writing a novel in a month sound easy.

"Step One: Write every day. Step Two: Make no excuse. Put your tail in the chair. Step Three: Do 1,667 words per day to reach your goal, but you know me—"

"Are we wimping out before we start?" Rose leaned back in her chair and took a drink of coffee. "Huh?"

"I'm not quitting, but you are fun to watch when you get riled.

Your face squinches up and your chubby cheeks don't know what to do with themselves. They sit there and jiggle. Here, let me show you."

Rose watched her friend as she pinched her own cheeks. Before she jiggled them, Betsy started to giggle. When she came up for air, she tried to speak. Again, no discernable words came out.

Complete control left Betsy's living room. Any talk of writing a novel, jiggly cheeks or anything else for that matter stalled for a good five minutes. Rose stood and in as stern of voice as she could muster, after getting control, she announced, "Put a lid on it and let's pray."

Rosie didn't wait for a response from her friend. She sat back down and lifted her voice to heaven. Afterwards Betsy chuckled and said, "If I can't write the Great American Novel after that prayer, I better hang my computer out to dry and find another passion."

"That's why God assigned you to me. You're my lot in life. I must till the soil until it's ready."

"You are so—"

"So spiritual. I know. Someone's got to do it."

"Not the words I was going for, Rose, but it'll work. Promise me you'll pray and give me a daily kick in the pants to get my words done."

"You can count on it." Rose got up. "How about we go over and tell Mary. I'm sure she'll want to hound you on your endeavor too."

"Oh goodie. I can't wait to have two of you needling me."

\*\*\*

The next morning, Rose carried her job of pestering her friend a bit too far when she said, "You should buckle yourself in the backseat with Matilda. Then you can type, type, type on your novel. Get some words down."

The evil eye Rosie received told her the caffeine hadn't tempered Betsy's morning mood yet and comments should be kept to herself. Rose chanced one more. "Bets, our next stop, which is Bushnell, Florida, is," Rose stopped to check Google. "It is three hours from here. Plenty of time to get hundreds of words written."

"If you're not careful, I'm going to make you ride with me.

Buckle you in and see how that works for you." Betsy hugged her and turned and walked towards their truck.

Rose jumped in their motorhome and pondered her friend's proclamation while her husband pulled out of the RV Park. No, riding in the back of anything moving down the freeway, not even a possibility in her case for a number of reasons.

The number one being, she wanted to keep her breakfast, lunch or dinner. Depending when their travels took place. The second reason: front seat to keep her eyes on the road ahead, making sure Larry paid attention to signage and hazards along their way.

Something she'd learn when Larry or one of the dealerships gave her driving lessons after they got to Ft. My—"

"Rosie, we'll be getting into the RV Park early today. There's a Wal-Mart next door. It's time you had your first lesson."

*How does he do it?*

"Hon, is there one of those caption thingamajigs over my head?" Rose questioned her husband before she checked it out for herself.

"No, but you've been planning Betsy's life all morning, figured I'd get your motor running too. Announcing it beforehand will give you time to write down all the excuses you have for not driving. Then we can use the paper to line the cabinets and drawers in our new place." Larry's chuckles filled the cab of their Class C.

Not even the angels assigned to the Pearly Gates could keep her tongue from expounding on what her hubby said. But first, she had to take care of the vibration coming from her phone, which she'd laid on the dash.

"The words are flowing."

"You've got this," Rosie answered back.

"Who's got what?"

"Betsy's putting pen to paper. Or in her case—fingers to keys. WOOHOO!"

Rosie settled back in her seat and the urge to voice a rebuttal to Larry's earlier comment vanished. Instead she said, "Mr. Wilford, the sky's the limit."

***

The following morning, on their final leg of their journey, Rosie had only one recourse to calm the ants in her pants. Sing

along with the radio. She'd fiddled with the buttons until she found
KLOVE and praised the Lord while Larry drove the last thirty
miles to Ft. Myers.

Rosie also prayed, making sure all the saints in glory land
heard. "Lord, I'm not sure what You have in store for us, but we're
ready for our next adventure. Thank You for everyone we met in
Mississippi and for Betsy's mom finding us a place to park in
Florida. Cypress Grove RV Park here we come. Amen."

"I'm with you. Those pictures Fran sent of the place were
quite impressive. Lots to do."

"And, after we settle in, Larry, the pooch and I are going to
start walking. I'm not sure, but if I'm not mistaken, my rear end
has expanded three sizes since we left Texas."

"No chance I'm commenting on that one."

"Smart man and, by the way, one who's turned into an
excellent driver."

"Dear, you got out of driving last night, but you're still going
to learn how to drive this thing."

"I know you don't believe me, but I did stub my toe last night.
I'm still getting used to our tinier space. Anyway, when we get
down to Ft. Myers, I've decided I want Ben to teach me all he
knows about driving."

"Glad to hear it. My blood pressure will stay in range and
there'll be no chance of me getting arrested."

"Good point, but you will be sorry if you miss the teaching
moment. There is something I need to tell you, which should have
hit me months ago." Rosie paused to get the words right.

"We're less than a half hour from our destination. Are you
going to tell me?"

"If you hush, I will."

"Sorry."

"I read something on Facebook yesterday. It said, 'Do
something scared.'"

"Huh?"

"Larry, I've known for a long time that I'm not trusting the
Lord in this not-getting-behind-the-wheel situation. If I believe for
one minute that I'm going to wake up one day and not be scared of
driving, I'm nuttier than I think I am. It's not going to happen. It's
like sewing. You don't make a wedding dress the first time you sit

down to sew."

"Makes sense."

"Can you forgive me for not having this epiphany sooner? Oh my goodness, I used one of Betsy's words." Rose chuckled.

"Hon, I forgave you awhile back about not driving. Whenever you're ready to learn, I'll be happy to take you out. I will be sad giving up the wheel. I like driving our new home."

"This is why I love you so much, Mr. Wilford."

"Breaker 21. We'll take Immokalee/Six Mile Cypress exit. Right lane and an immediate left."

"Thanks, Ben."

Rose loved to see Larry smile. At that moment his grin stretched clear across his tanned face. She adored the man the Lord had given her and prayed every day that he'd stay around for many more years to come.

For whatever reason, her thoughts went back to her expanding rear quarter. Rose glanced over at her hubby and concluded he'd put on a little weight too. Around his mid-section. *If I want him to be around, we need to make changes. Right this minute.*

"Larry, we're fat."

Her husband's smile faded and he said, "Can we talk about our pudginess later? Right now we're stuck in traffic."

"Okeedokie."

Rose relaxed and took in the sights of Ft. Myers. Her favorite thing of all greeted her on both sides of the highway. Palm trees. The fronds waved in the breezes as if to welcome them to their fine city.

Larry followed the others and in less than twenty minutes he pulled into the Cypress Grove RV Park and said, "Welcome home, Rosie, for at least the next three months."

Again gigantic palm trees lined the road they traveled into the park. After they checked in, Larry parked their smaller abode. Along with staying quiet while he backed in, Rosie zipped it when she spied the screened gazebo next to their concrete pad.

Strings of lights blanketed the roof of theirs, and the ones on the other lots too. Rose imagined what the structures looked like at night. Pure magic, for sure.

Larry worked on hooking their motorhome up and Rose quit daydreaming about the lights and took Baby out. They joined

Matilda and Betsy at the rear of their units and they took their pooches for a stroll.

"How does Baby like her new home?"

"Even though it's smaller, Bets, she seems happier. Slap me and call me purple."

"How's the…" Betsy hesitated then said, "Her bark—"

"Betsy, there's no need to shy away from the elephant in the room. Or, in our case, dog in the RV. It's a miracle. She's hardly barking at all. Who knew getting her a tinier RV would calm her down."

"Glad she's doing better."

"So are we. Don't want to get us kicked out of this fantabulous park. Need to give your mom an extra big hug for finding this one."

"I can't wait to check it out, but first we have a lunch date with her. I texted her on the way here and she was heading to a dance class. Said to tell everyone she wanted us all to come over to her place at 1:00."

"Can't wait to see her. It's been too long." Rose looked over at Mary when she'd joined them on their walk and said, "You will love Betsy's mom. She's a lady sold out to the Lord and isn't a bit reluctant to share her faith with others."

"Kind of like her daughter and best friend."

"Not even close, Mary. Not even close. Which reminds me, Bets, how's your writing coming?"

"I hit ten words over the goal when Ben pulled in the park. I wished I'd tried typing as we cruised down the road before. I fasten the seatbelt and I'm sitting back creating cleverness on my 'puter screen. Thanks for the idea, Rosie."

"Whatever it is you're doing. Keep doing it. I can't wait to read it."

"In due time."

"Mary and I can proof what you have so far. How about it?"

"How about we get off the subject of my book and onto Everly. When are they coming to Florida?"

"She called last night and said they'll get here on Friday night after Thanksgiving and will stay with her aunt in Naples. This gives her time to get settled and enroll Olivia in her new school. Everly's new job starts the middle of January."

"Hope her daughter's okay with the move. I always hated the first day of school after we relocated in the summer."

"So did I, Mary. It's not easy being the new kid. You never seem to fit in."

"Never had to experience moving to a different school myself. I spent all twelve years in the same town and graduated with some of the same kids I started kindergarten with." Rose smiled at the memory.

"And, that's why when Everly and her daughter get to Florida, Rosie, me and Mary will share our stories with Olivia. Show her how well we turned out after the years we spent moving around the country."

"Can't wait to hear what you two have to say. And now I understand why neither one of you have a smidge of empathy for me. Let me give you an exam—"

"Rosie, I think this would be a really good time for Mary and me to come clean. We don't care one iota about you." Betsy snorted this time, which caused even more laughter from the three of them.

Finally stares from other residents caused Rose to point in the direction of their RVs and she said, "It's time to hide in one of them before the park tells us to unhook and move on."

They hurried inside Rosie's RV. Their conversation returned to Olivia, and Mary said, "You do know we were kidding with you out there. We love you, Rosie. Don't we, Bets?"

"I guess so."

"What? I thought I was the lone person in this group who gave a hoot about my fellow man. And, speaking of caring about others, Betsy, it'd be a good idea to check on your dog. Not sure she's supposed to chew through her leash."

Betsy dropped the part of the leash she held and said, "Matilda, you're going to have to figure out how to make some money. This is the third one of these you've ruined since we started traveling."

"I'm sorry, Mom."

Rose tried to talk like she'd heard Ben and Betsy do, but it sounded more like a squeaky wheel than what she'd planned in her head.

"You could use some practice or WD40. One or the other."

Betsy laughed.

Mary headed to the door and said, "I need to scoot and set up the trailer. Since we're here for a while, I want to unwrap my twelve-piece place setting of china."

"China?"

"It's about all I found after the flood and I'm going to use it. Not save them for a special occasion. Like I did before. We're dining in style."

"Your dishes will come in handy at the reception when Everly and Douglas get married."

"Let's get them together and him down here before we're planning their future."

"I'm saying you—"

"I'm saying you're matchmaking." Bets joined Mary at the door. "I need to go write more words. When it's time to head to Mom's, we'll meet outside. I'm sure after lunch she'll want to show us around the park and introduce everyone to us. The infamous Early Birds.

*Betsy, we are a legendary bunch.*

## CHAPTER SEVENTEEN

For the next two weeks Betsy's mom took the Early Birds around and introduced them to everyone she knew at Cypress Grove RV Park. Seemed Fran had a friend everywhere they went. At the beach. At church. Or when they went out to eat.

Larry decided they fit in with the other Snowbirds when they volunteered to cook hotdogs and bratwursts on Thursdays at the main building. Or, maybe, their thinning and/or graying hair got them in the inner circle. He didn't know which one.

"With Turkey Day two weeks away, Larry, we need cooks and bottle washers for our afternoon feast," Joe shouted across the expansive grill.

"Where do we sign up?"

"Over there." Joe pointed the tongs at the office across the street. "They close at noon, you know."

"Didn't know that."

"You do now."

They served the last of the dogs and cleaned up. At 11:55 Larry put his rag in the basket and ran over to the office and put their names on the list. He hesitated on adding the women and told the receptionist, "I'm not sure, but I'll probably be back to add a few more."

"The more the merrier."

"Now it's off to Pickle ball."

"Have fun."

As Larry walked back across the parking lot, he questioned why he'd shared their afternoon activity with the woman behind the counter. The only explanation, his wife and friends made him socialize more.

"If I don't get out among the living, the other Early Birds will come and get me out of my trailer."

"Or they'll catch you blabbing with yourself," Rose rode up to him on her bicycle and stopped next to him. "Are you okay, or do I need to have the doctor check you out again?"

"I'm fine. Standing out here enjoying life."

"It appears so, but I'd suggest next time you want to talk to yourself out in public, cover your mouth. I don't want your mental state to be the topic of conversation at water aerobics in the morning."

"As my mom used to say, 'At least when they're talking about you, they're leaving someone else alone.' Anyway, where you headed?"

"Bets, Mary, Fran and I are going to check out some second-hand stores. I'm feeling the itch to get going on some volunteering again. This resting and relaxing is for old people and I ain't old."

"You could have fooled me."

"If you want to live to see tomorrow, you'll go talk with the guys and find us a place to help here in Ft. Myers. It's time."

"It's the start of the holiday season."

"Can't think of a better time." Rose got on her bike, but before she peddled off she said, "Not sure you know this, but Pickle ball won't save souls. Gotta go."

Larry watched his wife ride off, and then he saw she came to a stop in the middle of the road and put her kickstand down and walked back to him.

"Rosie, what are you doing?"

"You didn't ask, but Betsy's word total is 23,333 as of 9:30 this morning. Need to keep praying."

"You do know you're nuts?"

"I've been told I fit that description. We'll walk down that road together."

Larry chuckled as his wife headed back to her mode of

transportation. They did need to find opportunities to help in the community. After Pickle ball he'd call the number Pastor Steve gave them before they left Biloxi.

***

The next morning Larry called the phone number for the church. Their answering machine said, "We are closed on Friday. Please visit our church on Sunday at 8:30 and 11:00."

He shut his phone off and made a note of the service times. Next on his agenda, find out who else wanted to hit the beach. Maybe find breakfast.

Larry went out and knocked on Ben's RV first. When his friend came to the door, he said, "I don't know about you two, but I'd love to go to Ft. Myers Beach today. We can pile into my rig...or—"

"Or, I can drive. Go wake up Jeff and Mary and let's go find some water."

At 9:15 they all piled into Ben's truck and off they went in search of some surf and sand. Close to an hour later, after waiting in line to get over the bridge, his friend found a place to park his dually.

When Rosie planted her foot on the sand a minute later, she said, "Will you look at all these shells?"

"I'm in shell heaven." Betsy reached down and picked up a handful. After picking out a few, she put them in her jacket pocket.

"Careful, Bets, a creature could be living in one of those seashells."

Larry didn't know if his friend's jacket would survive its quick unfurling, but Betsy got it off and all the shells she'd collected lay back on the sand where they'd washed ashore before they'd arrived.

"I didn't mean to scare you, but I don't want you to stick your hands in your pocket and get the bejeebers scared out of you."

"Much appreciated, Lar. Hope no one saw me dancing around."

Once the laughter died down Ben said, "Hon, I'm pretty sure a half a dozen cameras flashed while you were doing your little jig. You're a Facebook sensation by now."

"You are such a funny guy."

"He's not kidding." Rose took out her phone. "See."

145

A snort followed and Betsy came over and slapped Rose on the arm with her flip flop. "You're lying to me."

"I am, but I loved your bug-eyed expression and how fast you came over to check to see the video."

"You'll pay dearly for that one, Rosie." Betsy wiped her feet off and put her shoes back on.

"How about we stop for breakfast? Someone at the park told me there's a place we can get great cinnamon rolls."

"Can we walk?"

"I'm not sure how far it is, but I'm sure we can make it."

A short time later they waited in line at the Magnolia Cafe. The aroma surrounding them almost made Larry cut in line and grab the whole pan of the sweet morsels, sitting on the counter. But he waited and watched the person drizzle frosting on top of all of them.

"Are we going to order or stand in line drooling on them?"

His wife's voice jolted him back to reality and he ordered two rolls and a coffee. The cashier gave him a plastic number to set on their table and they went outside to wait for the other four.

Rosie sat down at the picnic table and took out her phone. In less time than it took to blink her eyes, the results appeared. She grimaced at the findings, but couldn't wait to share the not-so-good news with her friends.

"Is this seat taken?" Mary asked as she headed down the stairs. Jeff followed behind her, carrying enough napkins to mop up Niagara Falls.

"Not sure we need that many, but always good to be prepared." Rose let go with one of her famous snorts then added. "And when I tell you the little tidbit I found, we're going to need them to sop up our tears."

They all stared at her and in the end Larry asked, "I don't want to know, but I'm sure these two are dying to know what's cooking in that brain of yours. Go ahead, Rosie."

"Get those napkins ready 'cause what I'm about to tell you will lose me some friends. The cinnamon rolls we're about to consume are 723 calories and 84 grams of fat each."

"Thus concludes the enjoyment factor of said delight."

"Sorry, dear."

"Don't repeat this to Ben and Betsy. We'll share it with them after the fact."

"Deal." Mary smiled.

"Number 7 and 8. Your order is ready. Also 9."

Before Larry made it to the door, Ben and Betsy carried out a tray laden in a mess of delectability, smothered in enough frosting to coat the outside of the building they sat next to.

Rosie, along with everyone else at the table, savored every last morsel of the roll. After her last bite, she picked up her paper plate and used her index finger to get every drop of frosting off of it.

After she accomplished that task she turned to Ben and Betsy and asked, "Want to know the cal-o-ries in what you—"

"You better be zipping it shut, Rosie. Remember, cal-o-ries don't count when you're out with friends on the beach. Same as on your birthdays."

"If by chance they did have cal-o-ries, we consumed almost eight hundred smackers in the last five minutes."

"Larry, I can't believe you stole my thunder."

"It sounded better coming from me." Larry took their trash and threw it in the container. When he came back to the table he said, "How about we walk back to the truck and never, ever come near this place again?"

"Lar, I'm with you. We need to volunteer more and eat less."

"All in favor of what Ben said."

Rose watched everyone's arm shoot up in the air. "It's unanimous."

"When we get to the RVs, let's have our first Early Birds meeting in Florida. Brainstorm some ideas, along with the list of places Steve gave us. I tried the church this morning, but they weren't open." Larry moved toward the sidewalk.

"Wait. While we're at it, I need some help brainstorming on my novel. I've hit the end of the second week and my brain is lagging behind on ideas."

"I've got an idea for you. I found it on Google and it could help you. Immeasurably." Rose took out her phone again and waved it around. "It is sure to give Betsy more things to write about."

"Whatever it is, it better not have to do with food."

Larry tried to catch Rosie's phone in midair, but she moved quicker than he did and she stuck her arm behind her back.

"If Mr. Wilford will leave me alone, I'll show all of you what I found."

"Lar, it's best if you leave her be. Let her show us her latest find." Betsy joined Rose on the sidewalk.

"Bless you, my dear. As I was saying before someone interrupted me, the women need to get on the road again. Or in this case, the three of us need to fly to Mitchell, South Dakota to see the Corn Palace.

"All their murals are made out of ears or husks of corn. See, there's one of Willie's face." Rose turned her phone for everyone to see the entertainer's picture. "Bets, this will give you lots of inspiration. Betsy? Mary? Who's heading north with me?"

"No one's going anywhere with you, unless it's back to the RV Park. And, dear, do you think these things through before you share them with us?"

"Apparently not. Only trying to help Betsy's writ—"

"You can help her in Florida. There's no corn on any of our horizons."

"Other than the cornball comments coming out of her mouth."

"See, I told you. Betsy always has to have the last word."

"Do not."

"Do too."

"Ladies, people are starting to stare. Can we move on?" Jeff laughed as he and Mary walked toward the crosswalk.

Rose followed, muttering under her breath. "Sad state of affairs when I can't add a little spice to our travels."

"Instead of spice, you're adding 'corn' to our comings and goings," Betsy poked Rosie's arm then added, "And, for the record, your idea will make it in my book. Priceless."

"Glad someone liked it."

"Hon, how about we add the Corn Palace to our itinerary when we do the northern states? Sometime in our future. Oh, I guess I better ask the other Early Birds. See if it's okay."

"Fine with Betsy and me."

"Us too. I'm dying to see a bunch of corn."

"It's a go then. Can we cross the street now?"

Once the six of them made it across Estero Boulevard, Rose stopped them again and said, "Early Birds, it's not the destination, it's finding people we can help along our journey. Those experiences, and one's we've already had, will give Betsy plenty to write about."

"Rosie, so far today, you've given me lots of fodder."

"Always happy to help. Now it's time to find someone else to help." Rose tucked her phone in her back pocket and asked the group, "Are we ready?"

"I was born ready."

"Me too."

"Me three. Don't forget about the proposed name change. I'm still voting for Southern Fried Birds." Jeff laughed as he put his arm around his wife.

"I vote for Taco Bell Birds."

"You would, Ben. How about we call ourselves the Southbound Birds, especially since we're in the South?" Rose accentuated the last word with the best southern drawl she could muster.

"Sold."

"Larry, we didn't vote."

"Don't need to, dear. Everyone is nodding their heads."

"Southbound Birds, it is…that's until we head out on our next adventure."

"Rosie's got a point."

***

"Hon, can you come inside for a minute?"

"What do you need?" Larry gazed up from the chaise lounge to find Rose blocking the sun he tried to get a suntan from.

"After our Early Birds, oh I mean Southbound Birds meeting, I asked Ben to bring over the final boxes out of our 5th wheel. I hoped they'd motivate me. One has your name on it. You need to come in. Make sure I'm not giving away something you want."

Larry stood and turned to his wife. "I hope you're taking your time. Not getting rid of anything you'll want later?"

"Mary and Betsy came over after our meeting. They held things up. It helped to put my things into perspective. How many pairs of tennis shoes do I really need?"

"If you toss or donate something, and you want it later, I'm not going to replace it," He tried to sound tough, but knew he talked to the wind when he said it. Her response verified it.

"Don't you worry about it, Mr. Wilford. If I need something, there's always another thrift shop or second-hand store open and ready to sell me anything I want."

"Where's the volume switch?" Larry attempted to lift the side of Rosie's shirt as they walked into their RV, only to get his hand slapped away. He tried again and said, "It must be here somewhere."

"You're getting on my nerves and so you know, nothing can turn me off."

"Not even God Himself." Larry cracked up until he saw his wife's frown.

"As I was getting ready to say, we found a second-hand store the other day. It doesn't hold a candle to Linda's place in Biloxi, Mississippi. The funny thing, the lady who works there said the property is For Sale."

"Why is that amusing? You're not in the market to buy anything."

"Says who?"

"The person who bought a new RV and plans on driving it around the USA with her significant other."

"Oh, I'm not buying it for us to take care of."

Larry gave his wife a sidelong glance and said, "You are right, Rosie. We're not buying anything."

"Sweetums, I thought since we're here in Florida for such a long time, we could work with the woman who runs the store. Get Linda involved. We can't forget Everly's coming in for a few weeks. I know how much she'd love to help."

"None of this tells me why you're wanting to buy the place. Betsy would tell you this is another time you're getting the cart before the horse. Trust me on this, we're not in the market for a store. Of any kind."

"Can't fault me for dreaming, but I'm married to a poop head." Rosie walked back out the door they'd entered less than five minutes before.

"I'll go through the box, dear." Under his breath he mumbled, "before she comes back in here and throws it all away."

Larry wondered how his wife came up with her outrageous ideas. Let alone believe it was a sensible thing to announce, out of the blue, that she wanted to buy a business? In a place they'd been at less than a month.

Only Rosebud.

While he went through his clothes, Larry turned on the local news. The anchor came on and talked about their upcoming segment and he yelled outside, "Rosie, you need to see this."

"What?" She pressed her nose to the door.

"The news."

"You know I'm not a fan of the nightly news or the news, in general."

"This, my dear, will interest you and the other ladies. Come on in."

As Rose took a seat on the couch, the reporter in the field asked, "What will you be doing?"

"We'll help women get a job. Teach them how to dress for success. Hovington Estates can stand for the betterment of their citizens, not the violence. The Lord has put it on my heart to help the women here in this community. The change starts now."

"Told you it would interest you," Larry said as he watched Rosie get out her phone and text.

"You bet we're interested. Goes with what I proposed earlier. Lar, we better hold onto our hats. God is up to something."

Larry nodded. He hoped it didn't include owning a piece of property in Ft. Myers, Florida.

## CHAPTER EIGHTEEN

"They're here. They're here." Rose clicked on the message on her phone the next morning.

Larry rolled over in their bed and asked, "Who's here?"

"Everly and Olivia. She texted and they're at the gate. Get dressed and take your bike down to let them in. I'll go tell the others."

Rose put on an array of pieces she grabbed out of her closet and ran over to Betsy's. After she knocked and sort of yelled, "Wake up in there." She went to Mary's and did the same thing.

Larry, Everly and Olivia got to their RV site and parked. Rosie rushed over and made sure she tempered her screams since their friends arrived at 8:00 am on Saturday morning.

"I can't believe you're here already." Rose gave her one of her Texas-size hugs.

"Rosie, let the poor thing breathe."

"Sorry."

"My aunt isn't doing well, so I needed to get down here and help her while I have the time off."

"What about your job?"

Rose noticed that her hubby gave her one of his looks when she asked. Yes, she was nosy. No crime in it.

"I can telecommute."

"Fantastic."

The arrival of the other two ladies turned into a hug fest. Rose turned to Larry. "Why don't you guys run and get us all bagel sandwiches. The brochure is on the table. The girls will stay here and catch up."

Larry stretched out the sides of his sweat pants. "Can I get dressed first?"

"Thought you already were." Betsy laughed then added. "I've been over to your house. You were wearing the same Denver Bronco t-shirt, sweats and slippers that time too."

"I'm going in to change. After that, I'll be ready to do your bidding." Larry laughed.

"I'll do the same."

"Thanks Ben." Rose took a peek at Jeff. "Well?"

"Picky! Picky! Picky! I thought I was looking good."

Mary pushed her husband toward their RV. "Go get changed, dear. Don't want you scaring little ones when the 'Jolly Green Giant' walks in and gives his order."

"I like my Green Bay Packer—"

"I know, but please don't share it with the world."

Rose enjoyed watching her friends and hubby early in the morning. From the expressions on Everly and Olivia's faces, they loved it too. Smiles all around and plenty of chuckles going on in the circle.

"I'm not glad my aunt isn't feeling well, but I'm so happy to see you ladies again and be a part of your family. Even for a little while."

"We are too, sweetie."

Rose wanted to ask about Douglas, but kept her trap shut. They'd have time to discuss any new developments in the budding romance in the days to come. For right now, they'd sit at the picnic table and chit chat about anything and everything.

"Rose tells me that you're writing a novel, Betsy. Did I hear her right? You're doing it in a month? I'm not sure that's possible."

"I am working on it. So far I'm staying on track, but reading over it—it's beginning to resemble a very loooooooong synopsis with lots of unnecessary words."

"Doesn't matter if it's filled with superfluous words…I do

love that word. Or if they're superb. It's up to the man upstairs what stays and what goes in your manuscript."

"Rosie, you do have a way with words and, yes, the Lord has lots to get rid of and gaps He will help me fill in when I get to editing.

"Then you'll let others read it to give you input, won't you?" Mary took a drink from her mug.

"If you stay around here too long, you'll hear the song *On the Road Again* more than you thought your nerves could take."

"Hey, it's only a couple times a day."

"A couple of dozen times."

Everly laughed and turned to her daughter, "Honey, it's a country song. Came out a long time before you were born.

"I love Willie's song. It's a classic."

"Go figure."

The men came back and from the sacks they carried, they'd purchased enough bagels sandwiches to feed the whole park. Two times over.

"We didn't know what our guests liked, so we bought some different kinds."

"I'm a vegetarian."

Rosie ran through in her mind every morsel in her refrigerator. Nothing in it would appeal to a teenager.

*What do we do now?*

"Olivia, come with me. I've got some yogurt in my RV. Is strawberry okay?"

Mary came to the young girl's rescue and when the two of them went over to get it, Rose glanced in Everly's direction. Sadness met her gaze and something she couldn't put her finger on. Almost a panic.

*The move?*

"Everly, what kind of sandwich do you want?" Rose took them out of the sack and read what was inside of the parchment paper.

"Canadian bacon sounds good."

The others retrieved their breakfast and sat around the fire pit, chatting with each other. Rose grabbed the one Everly asked for and the bacon for herself before going to sit next to her friend.

"Rose, I'm sorry for Olivia being a pain."

"She's a teenager. Aren't they supposed to be contrary on every subject known to man? Whenever they see fit?" Rose patted her arm. "Didn't have any of my own, but I've heard they turn into space aliens on their thirteenth birthday."

"That's about right. This move hasn't helped, but it's an answer to so many of my prayers. She has to see that."

"I've also heard they're blind until they hit twenty-five. But the Lord's got this."

"Thanks for the reminder and that's why we're here. I needed my new friends."

"We're here, Everly. No worries…except for one thing."

"What's that?"

"Your daughter can talk to me about giving roast beef the boot, but she can't ever make me eat yogurt."

After Everly quit laughing she said, "I don't mind it, but make sure you get the vanilla. The plain will prompt you to pray for the Lord's return so He can help get the putrid taste out of your mouth. Only thing that would work. Toothpaste doesn't cut it."

"Girl, you're going to fit right in. We're all waiting for His triumphant return, but while we're in the holding pattern, we've got things to do. How about we join the ladies at the picnic table and talk about a few things?"

*\*\**

Over the next three days, the Early Birds prepped for Thanksgiving and talked about the story on the news and how they'd help them. The ladies also made two trips to the second-hand store. Everly and Olivia tagged along.

After one of the visits, Rosie called the owner of the building to find out how much he wanted for it. When he told her she said, "You're way off, Mr. Waverly."

"Mrs. Wilford, prices are back up in Ft. Myers."

"Warehouse space, in your location, isn't. I've checked. You need to come down another $50,000. We'll talk more after the holidays."

Rose almost laughed when she said it and could almost hear Larry's head explode at her boldness.

*But we've got to get this going. And I need to call Linda. Get her take on all this.*

On the day before Thanksgiving, Rose texted Everly to come

155

over to Cypress Grove at 9:00 in the morning. Then she sent a message to Betsy and Mary, "Meet me in the clubhouse in a half hour."

***

"What is so important that we can't meet in one of our houses?"

"Bets, we can't let the guys know yet."

Everly arrived and asked, "Know what?"

"That I've talked to the owner of the building the thrift store is in. That I want to sell our house in Texas to buy it and call it Sassy Seconds Two. And that you're all looking at me like I've grown a third head."

"You're absolutely right on the last count."

"Mary, I appreciate your vote of confidence."

"I don't mean to say you're insane, but are you sure you want to sell your house?"

"After hearing the woman on the news last week and what we were able to do in Gulfport and Biloxi with those women. Proof is sitting right here in our midst." Rose touched Everly's shoulder. "I believe we can do the same thing down here in Florida."

"Have you called Linda?" Everly asked.

"I have," Mary said. "We've talked extensively, but not on this subject.

"About the plaques?"

Mary nodded her head. "Yes, my niece is interested in Linda's plaques. She asked her to send more pictures. Jennifer put them on her website, and as the saying goes, 'the rest is history'."

"So now she'll be busy creating her artwork, she won't be able to help us."

Rose scooted over closer to Everly. "Dear, I'll bet Linda will make time for this project. She told me other people help with them. Douglas being one of them."

The mention of his name caused Everly to smile. This made Rose almost want to break out in song. She didn't, and reminded herself not to go down the bunny trail of romance.

"Back to Linda. Let me give her a call and fill her in on what's going on he—"

"Put that phone down and stop right there, sister." Betsy stood. "Unless the Lord has written you a personalized note, saying

156

He wants you to buy this property. You, we, need to pray. It seems our practice lately has been to get the cart before the—"

"Have you and Larry been talking?"

"Nope, but we've got to be sensible."

"Okay, but can I call Linda and tell her about the idea? Even if we don't buy the property, we can still help the ladies. We do need someone in the business who knows how to do this sort of thing."

"Go for it."

"How about when she answers, we yell, 'Congratulations'?"

Rose put her phone on speaker and when Linda answered all of them, now sitting at one of the long tables, shouted their congratulations.

"Couldn't have done it without all of you."

"I know," Rose popped in. "Which brings us to something you can help us with. If you choose to."

"You name it."

Rose told Linda what she thought the Lord wanted them to do with the store in Ft. Myers. "I don't know about you, but wouldn't it be grand to have a Sassy Seconds Two?"

"I'd never thought about expanding."

"No time like the present. Oh, that's funny. We're about to celebrate Thanksgiving, then Christmas. Presents. Forget it. Didn't sound as special when I said it out loud."

"You're too funny, Rosie. How about I get back to you on what you've proposed? I need to get through the next few weeks. Then we'll talk."

"We'll work on this end and see what we can do."

Rose clicked off her phone and had six eyes staring at her. "I'm not going to do anything, that is unless Mr. Waverly calls me back."

"We need to have another Early Birds meeting."

Everly's eyes grew large and she asked, "What's an early bird?"

"What you've become a member of." Rose explained the significance of the name.

"I'm not sure I meet the criteria."

"You're here and you like us."

"I do. Guess I'm a member. When's the meeting? I need to leave soon to relieve Olivia."

"It'll be short. Ben will poo poo the idea until he checks the building. Once an architect, always an architect."

"Wouldn't expect any less of him, Betsy. How about you, Mary?"

"Since we're not putting any money in, Jeff or I don't have an opinion. Tell us when we're open for business and we'll show up to work."

"Don't encourage her."

"Bets, I'm going to put both Larry and you in the Poop-On-My-Parade room and close the door."

"Cart before—"

"The horse." Rose finished Betsy's reminder. "Mark my word, the Lord's working on the placement right now and I'm going to be the one in alignment with Him when all is said and done."

Rose stood and walked toward the door, continuing her conversation as she opened it, "We'll see what the men say. I'm counting on them to see my side."

Rosie had no idea why on this side of heaven she'd fathomed the three gentlemen taking her side, since one of them—her hubby, already gave his opinion on the matter. She hoped he'd change his mind and all the way back to their RVs she prayed like she'd never prayed before.

"I know what you're doing, Rose." Betsy came up to her with a grin on her face."

"You'd all do well to be doing the same."

"All three of us are rooting for your idea and yes, I've been praying…all along. You hinted at this the other day and I told Mom about it. She has alerted her prayer group. They're praying too. Sounds crazy, but stranger things have happened through the power of prayer."

"Want me to name a saved marriage, or two?" Rose saw Everly's confused expression and told her, "I'll tell you all about it after the first of the year."

"Hey, Ben, where's Jeff and Larry?"

"They're in fixing a healthy lunch."

"Please tell me it's not yogurt?"

"No, Rosie, it's sandwiches."

"I wished they'd hurry. I want to get the meeting going since

Everly has to leave."

"Meeting? Don't remember scheduling one."

"Benjamin, we're having a meeting to discuss a possible Sassy Seconds Two in Ft. Myers. I hope we'll be buying the property to house it."

"We'll be buying…what? Betsy?"

"Hon, our friend's reference to 'we're' is Larry and her. Not all of us. I believe she's including us to make sure we want to help in the venture."

"Is Rosie still talking about buying the second-hand store?"

"Yes, she is, Larry. Come out here. You too, Jeff. Take a seat. We're having ourselves an Early Birds/Southbound Birds meeting."

## CHAPTER NINETEEN

Larry listened to his wife's proposal and for the first time he heard her heart. Did he still think her a tad over the top? Yes. The part about them selling their home in The Woodlands and downsizing, made him sit straight up in his lawn chair.

But the rest made perfect sense. They wanted to help people and what Rose talked about fit the ladies to a tee. About moving to a smaller house, as he said when they traded in the 5th wheel and got the Class C, who needed so much stuff anyway.

With them spending less and less time in Texas, going smaller, or not getting another home could work and he said as much, "Rosie, I'm seeing where you're going."

"You do?"

"Larry, I'm even seeing it clearer." Betsy raised her hands to heaven and said, "If the Lord isn't in on this, I'm not a Bible-believing fool sold out to the Lord."

"We better invite our neighbors over." Mary messed with her phone and soon worship music wafted through the air. "Yes, we are about to jump into a full-fledged revival meeting in RV Spot #23."

"Hon, you're onto something here, however, we need to wait to hear back from Linda. I don't want to move ahead without her and the lady we saw on the news."

"Me either…as much as I hate to wait." Rose went over and gave Larry a hug then turned to Everly. "And you need to get home to your family."

"I'll be praying for this. The one in Mississippi helped me so much. I couldn't have landed the job here in Florida without all of you and your commitment to the cause."

"Will we see you tomorrow?"

"No, I'm cooking for the three of us. A little bit vegan and a whole lot of turkey and stuffing."

Rose walked Everly to her car and Larry overheard their exchange, which warmed his heart. His wife needed this woman as much as she needed Rosie.

"I'll be in touch. Happy Thanksgiving to you, Olivia and your aunt. Hope Mildred feels better soon."

"Thank you!"

Larry met Rose as she walked back and gave her a hug. He'd wait for what the Lord had in store for them, but he'd already seen a change in his bride. She loved the Lord with all of her heart and wanted nothing else than to do His will. No matter what.

*Where did all of her fear go?*

He couldn't answer the question, but stopped and glanced down at his wife. A single tear trickled down her cheek. Larry reached over and wiped it away and said, "A penny for your thoughts."

"They went up. They're worth a dollar or two in this economy." She smiled at her husband.

"Yours…they're worth at least five bucks." He reached into his pocket to get his wallet.

"Larry, I'm in awe."

"Of how much the price of your thoughts have gone up?"

"No, silly. I'm in awe of the Lord and I'm not sure why He put Everly in our lives the first time, but to do it a second time. Whatever the Lord has in mind, it must be good."

"We'll be on the front row when He does it."

"Larry Wilford, I love you."

"Even when I pop your balloons?"

"Even then and even more when you see through my craziness."

Larry pondered his question for a moment. Afraid he'd put

an idea in her head, but he plunged ahead, "The old Rosie, she'd be second guessing herself. Too afraid to move forward. What happened?"

"The Lord." Rose took her phone out and hit a few buttons. "Let me read you the verse I read this morning in 2 Timothy 1:7. *'For God has not given us a spirit of fear, but of power and of love and of a sound mind.'*"

"The sound mind part. I'm not so sure about."

"Bets, you do know how to ruin a moment, but I love you anyway and for the rest of you, thanks for putting up with me."

"Wouldn't be the same without you, dear."

"You're right about that. How about we go in to our RVs and get our side dishes ready for the feast tomorrow?"

"Always the taskmaster."

"Don't worry about it, Rosie. I made some extra ones," Betsy's mom said as she walked up to their RV spot.

The bright colors in Fran's flowered capris almost reached the seating area before she did. No one else in the crowd could pull off the outfit the older woman wore.

"You didn't have to do that."

"Rose, I'm thrilled to do it. And I'm so glad you're all here."

"What did you make us?"

"I see you haven't changed, Ben."

"Mom, when it comes to your food. I'm always hungry."

"Unlike the times I sit something in front of him—"

"Bets?"

"Thanks for stopping her in midstream, Mom. I gotta tell you. She's turned into quite a cook."

"I hear she makes a pretty good potato salad. I'll see if I can get the quote right, 'I think it's better than your mom's.'"

"Who told you I said that?"

Rose gave herself up and everyone joined in the good-natured fun. Larry agreed with his friend, Ben's mother-in-law made a plate of fried chicken that would make you admit you'd robbed the local bank when you hadn't.

"Hope you made your fried chicken, Fran. It's the best."

"No, Larry, that's on Sunday's menu. But your compliments will always get you an extra cookie. Why doesn't everyone come over? I made a batch of chocolate chip this morning. When you come home, you can bring the dishes I made for you."

Larry filed in behind Ben. The line appeared as if they followed the Pied Piper. When there was a cookie at the end of the trip, he'd dress as Bozo the Clown to get one.

"Hon, remember our diet?"

"I will, after I've eaten a half dozen, or so."

"In your dreams." Rose chuckled.

"Then you better be falling to sleep."

"Those two never change, do they?"

"No, Mom, they don't. That's why we keep them around."

They reached Betsy's mom's home and Larry admired the landscaping outside her double wide. A family of pelicans sat perched next to the stairs into her home. Seashells graced the flower beds. Along with three azalea bushes.

Larry stomach grumbled and everyone turned when Fran asked Rosie, "Are you starving this poor man? Get in here and let me give you a cookie. Do you want some milk too?"

"No, he's lactose intolerant."

"Thank you, Rosie, for letting all of Cypress Grove know my ailments."

"You're welcome. I'd rather they know so they don't feed you any either. It does bad thing—"

"We know all that." Larry took Rose's arm and led her to the table. "Come eat a cookie."

Larry savored every bite and wanted to steal his wife's too. While he contemplated the strategy to do such a thing, he saw Ben look at his wrist and asked him, "Are you going somewhere?"

"We need to head to the airport. Brian and Amy are coming in. They're staying until the middle of February."

"No 4-wheelers for us to ride, but I'm sure we'll find something to do." Larry glanced at his own watch. "If you're picking them up at 2:00, you better get a move on."

Fran gave each of them a glass dish filled with delicious looking food and instructed all of them, "Don't let me catch you eating any of it beforehand. We need every stitch of what's in those bowls."

"Yes, ma'am. Thanks for the cookies."

"You're welcome."

On the way back to the RV, Larry smelled the corn casserole.

He decided if he didn't hurry and put it in the refrigerator at home, he'd eat it right on Cypress Grove Drive.

Rose must have read his mind when she said, "If you lean that thing over anymore, it's going to spill. Carry it the way you're supposed to."

"I'm admiring her handiwork."

"No, you're trying to get a whiff of what's in there."

"Yep, I am."

"Carry it straight. Remember Fran will hunt you down if anything happens to her dish, or its contents."

Rose glared at Larry and he held the dish tight against his chest. No more worries of spillage or a chance tasting, if anything slopped out.

"Bets, I have loved getting to know your mom. Still can't believe she's in her late 80s. She makes great cookies too; which Larry ate almost all of."

"I did not." Larry laughed, taking another cookie out of his pocket.

"He's still at it. And, yes, Mom is pretty special. Oh, and Rose, before I forget to tell you, she wants to help us with the ladies at Hovington Estates. Since she worked in the corporate world, I'm sure they'll benefit from anything she can tell them."

"Sage advice from someone who knows how to cook."

"Don't know who's worse at thinking about their stomachs."

"Jeff, it's a toss-up." Larry rubbed his stomach and took another bite of cookie.

***

"Can I get rid of these leftovers, Larry? They been in here since Thanksgiving night and today is Monday. I'm not touching another helping of any of it."

"Don't blame you. If you put them in a bag, I'll take it to the trash. A walk would do me good since I'm sure I put the weight back on I lost."

Rose deposited the leftovers in a bag and gave it to her hubby. "There you go."

"What's on your agenda today. Want to take a bike ride?"

"I've got some phone calls to make."

"Are we waiting on the Lord?"

"I am, but it never hurts to remind people who you are." Rose picked up her phone and pushed some buttons.

"Dear, trust me on this one. No one will forget you after they've met you for the first time."

"That's the kindest thing you've said all day."

"It's 8:00 in the morning."

"Then you got an early start. Like I'm doing. Now get out of my hair so I can make some calls."

Rose called Marie at Hovington Estates and told her she'd been in touch with Carol at the second-hand shop and about their ongoing plans for the future.

"We are so excited you and the other two ladies came to Ft. Myers. But Rose, I'm not sure with Carol's health concerns, how much longer she can run the business."

"If we can find someone to come along side of her and take some of the load, I know it can work. That's why we've called our friend in Biloxi. Linda Richeson is…" Rose left the rest unsaid when Everly's name came to mind.

"Rose, are you still there?"

"I am, and I know someone who'd work with Carol. That is until after the first of the year. By then, Linda will be onboard."

"Sounds good."

Rose ended the call to Marie and decided to run the latest news by her friend, but when she called Everly, she stated, "I can't talk."

Loud voices sounded in Rosie's ear and she yelled into the phone to tell her friend she'd call her back. About the time Rose went to end the call, Everly came on and said, "I can't help you. I'll talk to you later."

"Okay."

Rosie shut her phone off and it was anything but okay and she decided when Larry got back, they'd take the RV and find out what happened.

## CHAPTER TWENTY

Larry walked in a half hour later and Rosie had her purse over her shoulder. She told him, while opening the RV door, "I've already asked Ben. We're taking his truck. There's something going on with Everly."

"Sit down, dear. We're not going anywhere."

Rose's phone beeped. She checked the text from Everly. It said, "I lost my job."

"We're going now." Rose gave Larry the phone on her way out the door.

"I'm right behind you."

GPS got them to the address she'd given them. Rose jumped out and headed to the house the minute Larry stopped the truck. Her friend met her at the front door.

"They said they've changed their mind and filled the position with someone else."

"Give me your phone. I'm calling these people."

"Rosebud?"

"Maybe I'm not. I cannot believe they'd let you go the Monday after Thanksgiving? Unbelievable."

*Please, Lord, let me have five minutes with one of the execs. I promise I'll repent after the call is over.*

"They contacted me when I got back here Wednesday night."

Rose clinched her fist and from the expression on Larry's face, he'd like nothing better than to talk to someone at the company himself.

"The sad part. I did some checking and I'm not sure I wanted to work for them anyway. They're in over their heads in debt and created a new corporation to get out of the monies they owe their employees and vendors."

"The Lord directed you to find this out before you got in the middle of all of it." Rosie smiled when another thought came to mind.

"I'm afraid to ask, dear, but why are you smiling?"

"Larry, the Lord's timing. This is Him directing our paths. Now Everly is available to work at the thrift store. It's meant to be. Don't you see it, Everly?"

"My bank account doesn't see anything other than red ink."

"Money is no issue, dear one. The Lord and I, we've got this covered." Mildred stood at the front door. She then stepped out on the porch and said, "Everly, I've haven't met your friends, but what you've told me, I'd listen to them. They're giving you an opportunity. I'd say, take ahold of the plan He has for you."

"Mildred, it's wonderful to meet you. And Everly…you need to listen to your aunt."

"I don't want to take her money."

"You're not taking anything you're not going to get when I'm dead and gone. Dear, you and Olivia are all I have left. Can't I share the Lord's bounty with those I adore?"

"She's giving you an offer you can't refuse, dear."

"Rosie watched *The Godfather* the other night. Now I can't do anything with her."

Everly laughed through her tears then looked at her aunt. "Aunt Milly, are you sure about this?"

"I am, sweetie." Mildred walked over and hugged her niece.

"Then let's get started, even if Linda doesn't come in and help us." Rose stepped up next to them and continued, "We can make a boatload of women's dreams come true. Can I get an amen?"

"Amen."

Rose spun around and saw every one of the Early Birds, or whatever they called themselves, standing on the lawn with grins on their faces. Ben's brother and sister-in-law and Betsy's mom also came along for the ride.

"Rosie, if you haven't noticed, Everly hasn't given you her answer yet."

"Cart before the—"

"Bets, I got this one." Rose turned back to Everly, "Do we have a yes that you'll help Carol run the store? Please! Please! Please! You can't beat the living arrangements."

"Who's staying where?" Linda pushed her way in. Right behind her stood Douglas.

"How did you know?"

"Everly, your Aunt Mildred texted us, but we were already on the outskirts of Ft. Myers when it came in."

"You?" Everly couldn't contain her laughter.

"Technology isn't only for younger people."

"Yes! I'll do it."

Rose smiled when Douglas came over and gave Everly, in Rose's estimation, a happily-ever-after hug. The crowd cheered, but a chorus of "Thank You, Jesus" sounded when Olivia went over and joined the party.

Another thought hit Rosie, "Linda, you reminded me of something I forgot to do. Bets, when we get back to the RVs, I have a present for you. It's perfect." Rose kissed her friend on the cheek and started to hum, *Jesus Loves Me.*

"Yes, Jesus, You do love and provide for all our needs."

"While you're praising the Lord, Rosie, you might want to answer your phone." Larry went and sat on the porch swing.

Rose grabbed her phone out of her pocket and sat next to her hubby, but a moment later she jumped up and mouthed the words she heard on the other end of the line. Larry must not have understood and shrugged his shoulders. Guess lip reading wasn't one of his fortes.

When the owner of the building let Rose speak, she said, "Mr. Waverly, we are still interested. We'll come to your office tomorrow and talk. Thank you. Thank you. Thank you." She hung up, hollered a hearty Hallelujah, and did a dance only she could do. The crowd cheered for a second time.

Within seconds the small porch took on the appearance of an overcrowded elevator. Rosie deduced that they'd congregated on it to hear the who, what, where and when. And as soon as she caught her breath, she told them, "Mr. Waverly's ready to sell."

"Then I guess we're ready to buy." Larry got up from the swing and hugged her.

"Well then, praise the Lord and pass the turtle soup."

## THE END

PS: FYI: Betsy Stevenson finished her novel. All 52,392 words. As she typed *The End* she said, "Let the editing begin."

Read Early Birds first chapter available below

# A CALL TO SALVATION:

My prayer while writing *Early Birds* and *Southbound Birds* was for my readers to come away knowing the Lord loves them and that prayer works. If you've finished reading and have never asked Jesus Christ into your heart, I'd like to give you the opportunity to do so today.

Lord Jesus, I'm a sinner and I repent of my sins. Please forgive me. I believe Jesus died for my sins and rose again on the third day. Please come into my heart and fill me with Your Holy Spirit. AMEN!

If you prayed this prayer, you probably have questions about what's next:

1) Find a good church that teaches the Bible.
2) Set aside time each day to focus on God by reading your Bible and praying.
3) Develop relationships with people. Try to find a friend in the church you attend who can help you spiritually.
4) Publicly proclaim your new faith in Christ and your commitment to follow Him by being baptized.
5) Check out this website: www.gotquestions.org. They are there to help you out.

Janetta Messmer is an author of two other books: *Early Birds* (Book #1 in the Early Birds series – Christian Comedy) and *Chords of Love* (a Historical – My Secret Love Collection).Visit her www.janettafudgemessmer.com. On Facebook (Janetta Fudge Messmer) or Twitter (@nettiefudge).

Early Birds Chapter One

CHAPTER ONE

"You want to do what in an RV?" Betsy couldn't believe her husband's pronouncement. And out of the blue, no less.

"I want to retire and travel around in an RV," Ben put down the morning paper as he repeated the bombshell. Then smiled when he reached down and picked up their 13-pound pooch. "Matilda, tell your mama you want to see the U.S.A. in a Chevrolet...or maybe a Ford dually, pulling a 5er."

*Lord, is this really You? An RV, of all things."*

Betsy could only stare at Ben after his out-of-character comment. Then she countered with, "But honey, you can't quit your job. You're only 59 years old."

"Matilda and I have been talkin—"

"Okay, Benjamin Stevenson, I've heard it all now. You're telling me you and our dog have been discussing our long-range plans." Betsy shook her head, hoping this would wake her up from the bizarre dream unfolding in front of her.

Ben placed his two hands on Matilda's black and white head and turned her to face Betsy. "Mom, you and Dad should quit your jobs and spend more time with me."

Betsy couldn't help but laugh at Ben when he pretended to talk through their newly-acquired Boston terrier mix.

"Matilda told me she wants us to retire, sell our house and buy an RV."

"And I'm going to take you to the doctor this afternoon." Betsy dried her hands on the yellow towel, hanging on the oven. "Because you've been working *way* too hard."

"That's exactly right and why I should quit my job so I can spend more time with my girls. Think about it. Now we can travel around in an RV with Rose and Larry."

Half of Betsy's insides shouted, "He's gone off the deep end." The other half screamed, "Hallelujah. My prayers have been answered. He's finally come to his senses and wants to quit his job."

"...and another thing, Bets, look at all the material our retirement and subsequent travels would give you for your writing."

Betsy nodded her head. "Mr. B. we'll discuss this later. Right now I need some time to think and pray about all of this."

"Important we get the Lord's take on it. I'll take Matilda out for her morning walk." Ben opened the front door and turned. "Betsy, so you know, I've been praying about this for a while. It's like He's putting everything into place."

*Except the part where you tell your wife what is going on.*

Betsy watched her husband close the door then rushed into her office. First thing on the agenda, call Rose. Her best friend, who'd been bugging them to hit the road, would want to know the latest development.

Ever since the Wilford's bought their 5th wheel a couple of years ago, they'd hounded them to get one too. Rose commented the other day, "Wouldn't it be fun—the four of us, crisscrossing this great land of ours?"

"Rosie, you might have gotten your wish."

The fourth ring told Betsy that Rose either lost her phone or ventured out for the day. No need to leave a message. Her friend would check in when she got back from who knew where. While Betsy had the phone in her hand she called her mom, getting the same result.

*No one's home for me to tell our earth-shattering news to.*

This time she left a message—a very vague one. No need to give her mom a heart attack. Betsy hung up and did her usual when exciting, or in this case, stunning news abounded. She flipped open her laptop and wrote in her journal.

Yes, she'd better document what went on, 'cause from the

sounds of things, there'd be plenty of things to write about. As Betsy typed, joy bubbled up inside of her. When she lifted her fingers off of her keyboard, she sat back in her office chair and marveled at the outrageous idea.

*Really, Lord.*

Betsy couldn't get over the fact what her hubby proposed fit exactly in what she'd hoped and prayed for. At least the part of Ben getting out of his job sooner than later. The RV part—not totally sold on it. Not sure she'd ever jump on the idea.

She recognized Ben needed out of his job or the stress would do him in. She'd listened for way too long how he and the others in the office battled with their CEO. Most times Mr. Greenspan shot down ideas saying, "I can see too much cost overrun already. Do a feasibility study."

Betsy commended her husband for sticking it out this long. Not that she hadn't recommended he get out when their marriage started to suffer. His response, "I can't. Gotta work until I'm 65. Can't retire on nothing."

Ben put in his time. Sometimes 80-plus hours a week. Betsy remembered she'd teased him once, "I'm going to make you a t-shirt that reads: Over-and-above-the-call-of-duty-kinda guy." Ben didn't find it funny.

"My love, you are the go-to guy. But after today's news, Mr. Greenspan will have to do it without you." Betsy chuckled. "When all we see is the impossible, God can and will do amazing things. I believe He did it today."

Betsy turned her attention back to her computer, scanning the words she'd typed. They needed a few tweaks, but for the most part they were perfect for her blog. Betsy copied and pasted the text and titled it: *PREPOSTEROUS PROPOSITION.* An apt heading for the announcement of the century.

Thinking about their Bible study group and her writer friends' reaction to their latest newsflash made her laugh. "They're not going to believe this. Oh, and their comments, I'm sure some will bring the house down."

Betsy reread her blog again. This time out loud.

Yes, I've been hit with a preposterous proposition and I'm not sure if I'm dreaming or my hubby is NUTS. Let me fill you in on what transpired. Ben waltzed into the breakfast nook, as he does every Saturday morning, but this fine day he announced. "Let's retire, sell our house and buy an RV."

Alrighty then!!! I'm glad I didn't have a mouth full of coffee when he made his big announcement. Or he'd been wearing it along with his sweat pants.

To say the least, I was surprised since my hubby's not one who springs things on me. Normally we talk things to death before we make a decision on anything. But not this time. He stated his case then told me he and the Lord (and Matilda) had been discussing it for quite some time.

I sat there stunned while Ben said things were falling into place. The funny thing is, I'm overjoyed with the idea (for the most part – an RV, I'm not so sure. ☺)

I've prayed for a long time for a change to happen. For both Ben and me to dream once again, like we used to. To trust in the Lord and His plans for our lives. To have the courage to step out in faith.

Today's proposition told me our Father has us on His radar. He cares for you and me. His love knows no bounds.

I'm sure there's more to come on this subject. I'll keep you posted.

Love ya!!!
Bets

PS: Sorry to break the BIG news without a warning. Hope you were all sitting down and hadn't taken a drink of anything. ☺

When Betsy finished reading the blog for the third time, she put it in the *Pending* file for a date one week later. She had to wait until Ben told his job about his upcoming retirement. Another reason: Didn't want the masses...*Yeah, right...*to read it before she told Rosie.

*Speaking of which, where is that woman when I have BIG news to tell her?*

~

Ben and Matilda strolled around the neighborhood and he couldn't remember a time he'd enjoyed their walk as much. He'd have broken out in a dance, but his neighbors might call the authorities.

But after he'd laid out his plan, he felt 50 pounds lighter and a couple inches taller. However, he should have prepared Betsy for what he'd been praying for over the last three months.

Never seemed a good time. Until today. This morning he decided to blurt it out and see what happened. Other than her shocked expression, Betsy handled it pretty well. Ben thought she might throw something at him since he blindsided her.

Similar to the way she... "And we all know how that worked out." Ben turned the corner. His pooch followed.

The spring in his step from earlier left him. Now all Ben wanted to do was take back all the nasty things he'd said to his wife when she announced, "I'm going to write for a living. Not find another job. I'll make money, Ben. You wait and see."

She didn't make money and that fact sent him into a complete meltdown. That and his job. He couldn't put his brain around it or her new career. Every chance Ben had, he made sure Betsy saw how unhappy her proposed plan made him.

"And now I expect her to understand my crazy idea of buying an RV and traveling. Even if we have the money to do it."

Ben turned down Locust Street and headed home. He had some explaining to do and hoped Betsy would open her mind to the possibilities. Then he laughed. No worries there. His wife, the dreamer, would grab on with both hands and run with it. That's why he'd married her in the first place.

"Hey Ben. Matilda."

When Ben's neighbor from across the street called his name, he knew he'd be tied up for a good half hour.

*If Betsy needs me, she'll call.*

He walked up to Jeremy and Matilda plopped down next to him. Almost like his pooch knew the conversation could take a while.

Made in the USA
Charleston, SC
17 October 2016